SPUD TACKETT
AND THE
ANGEL OF DOOM

ALSO BY ROBBIE BRANSCUM

The Murder of Hound Dog Bates

SPUD TACKETT
AND THE
ANGEL OF DOOM

BY
ROBBIE BRANSCUM

THE VIKING PRESS

NEW YORK

First Edition
Copyright © 1983 by Robbie Branscum
All rights reserved
First published in 1983 by The Viking Press
40 West 23rd Street, New York, New York 10010
Published simultaneously in Canada by Penguin Books Canada Limited
Printed in U.S.A.
1   2   3   4   5   87   86   85   84   83

Library of Congress Cataloging in Publication Data
Branscum, Robbie.   Spud Tackett and the angel of doom.
Summary: An evil evangelical preacher disrupts life
in an Arkansas farm community during the second world war,
affecting fifteen-year-old Spud, his grandmother, and cousin Leroy.
[1. Farm life—Fiction.   2. Evangelists—Fiction]
I. Title.
PZ7.B73754Sp 1983   [Fic]   82-13621   ISBN 0-670-66582-7

To Doree Stone for her understanding kindness.

To Diane Tilley, my friend and kinswoman.

*To all who have been scared silly by hellfire
and brimstone preaching.*

*Most of all to Ray, whose roses bloom
in my heart, on the hottest summer day
or the coldest winter night.*

CHAPTER
ONE

I didn't hate the Japanese people for starting the war because Grandma said that the common everyday folks, just like us, couldn't help having war, that it was our country's leaders who decided such, and that the folks like us and most of the Japanese people had to go along with it as best we could.

No, I didn't hate the Japanese—I was just mad, mad as hops at them for ruining Christmas. For all my fifteen Christmases, my uncles, aunts, and cousins came home to spend Christmas with Grandma and me—bringing cakes, and sacks of pumpkin, and raisin pies.

Grandma would roast tender frying chickens with sage and onion dressing, and we would feast and play the time away. This year there'd just be me and Grandma. Oh, I suppose there'd be the usual stocking with an orange, an apple, a pack of gum, and a candy bar for me, but somehow this year it didn't seem enough. Or maybe I'd outgrown the joy of it. I'd not tell Grandma, though. It'd shame her deader than a doornail to know the boy she'd raised was thinking of himself more than the boys of hers going to war— sons, sons-in-law, and some older nephews.

When I'd asked Grandma why the menfolks was going to war before they was asked or told to go, Grandma snapped, "Why, Spud Tackett, our Arkansas boys don't never wait till somebody throws rocks at 'em. They jest hop in an' does what needs doin'."

Grandma's eyes looked real proud, and, truth to tell, I felt sort of proud myself, and said, "I wont t' go too, Grandma. I ken shoot."

"I know ye ken, Spud, an' real good too. But big boys like ye need t' stay home an' keer fer the folks left behind—old folks like me an' little younguns."

I thought maybe Grandma was right about the little

younguns, but I had my doubts that Grandma needed me to take care of her, for she was pure whang leather, the strongest kind. The whole hills seemed covered with a brooding sadness as menfolks left for war. But the routine of farm work went on as always.

Then on Saturday it came the first snow of the year. As me and Grandma walked to church the next day, I noticed that every tree looked like a Christmas tree and even the worst old houses like a body dreams of living in.

There was mostly old folks in church and middling to young women with babies. Church was held in our little one-room school, but then everything was held in the school—from pie suppers to funerals. I always hated going to school for a few days after a funeral for, in my mind, I could still see the pine coffin at the foot of the platform where the teacher had her desk and Brother Rose his pulpit. I could 'most hear the kinfolks of the dead one saying how their loved ones looked so natural, just like they was sleeping. As for me, I'd rather dead folks looked dead, so if a body met them on a dark night, they'd know to start running.

I didn't pay too much mind to the preaching. I never did, just mostly looked out the window and wished I was outside. Besides, I was used to old Brother Rose's sermons—he'd been our pastor ever since I could remember.

Suddenly old Granny Treat yelled, "Glory to God! Praise the Lord! I done had me a vision."

My neck hair crawled, and I could see Brother Rose's eyes go wide 'cause folks didn't have visions often in our little Baptist church, and since it was the first time I could recall anyone interrupting Brother Rose's sermon, I sat up and listened, and so did everyone else.

Granny Treat was standing and looking sort of wild-eyed, her gray hair straying from the bun and snuff juice tracing itself in time grooves down her chin. Fact, her whole face was time tracks. Seeing she had folks interested, she yelled again, "I done had me a vision."

I heard my grandma snort plain as day, and Granny Treat must've heard it too 'cause she raised her voice even louder, yelling, "The Lord told me in a dream that a man of God is a-comin' heer, a-comin' heer t' the hills. An angel he be. He's a-comin' t' lead us through the war, t' lead us t' Glory."

With that, Granny Treat sat down. She looked smugly around at the open-mouthed folks and patted her straying hair snugly. Brother Rose had pulled himself together and said kindly, "Thank you, Sister Treat," and went on preaching.

With the excitement over, I went back to not listening again.

After church, when everyone had shaken hands and left but me and Grandma, Brother Rose said, "Now, I do wonder what brought on Sister Treat's vision," and his eyes looked like they were laughing. Grandma's eyes got all crinkly, too, and she said, "I expect it was 'cause of the letter she got yesterday from her grandboy sayin' he'd met a preacher who was headed this way holdin' revivals."

Brother Rose laughed out loud and said, "Well, I cain't think of no better way of spreadin' the news than havin' a vision in the middle of church."

"In a pig's eye," Grandma snapped, then laughed too.

I sure wasn't laughing the next day, though, 'cause we got a letter, or Grandma did, saying her youngest son's boy, Leroy, was coming to stay a spell. I had a hard time sleeping that night 'cause of things aggravating me fierce.

It was a plain fact I didn't know what to do. I mean, with a city cousin coming to live with us till times got better or the war got over with, it looked to me like Grandma wouldn't be too likely to let me have enough money for new shoes. She said we didn't have the money, but I knowed we had leastways thirteen dollars left over from the last year's berry picking. And when I said so, Grandma snapped, "Spud Tackett, ye know that money is fer hard times."

Far as I was concerned, times couldn't get much harder without plumb killing me. 'Sides, Grandma thought boys didn't have no business a-wearin' new shoes but once a year nohow.

I turned over and punched the lumps in the feather bed down flat with my fist, doubting I'd ever sleep no more. I mean, a cousin coming sort of made me look at everything, including myself, with new eyes— not that I'd ever been much to look at, mostly bones and hair held together by freckles. Grandma said I took after Pa's side of the family. I wouldn't know 'cause I'd never seen Pa. He'd been killed someplace way off 'fore I was born. For that matter, I couldn't recall Ma much neither, 'cause she left the farm when I was real little, about three years old. I reckon that was about twelve years ago, but I suppose she looked like Grandma, I mean her being her daughter and all.

Truth to tell, looking like Grandma wasn't saying

much neither, 'cause she was worn to a strip of rawhide by the Arkansas weather and farm work. Her eyes were a snapping blue, and her voice had a sting that could nigh flay a body when she got a mad on. Her white hair flew around her head like cotton candy, and outside she wore Grandpa's britches, 'cept on Sundays.

Sometimes I thought Grandpa hadn't died at all, just sort of turned into Grandma, but reckon maybe it was 'cause of her wearing his clothes and hat and she was allus saying what Grandpa would say or do if he hadn't went on.

Grandma always acted like Grandpa was cut down in the prime of life, but he was ninety-seven when he died four years ago, and Grandma was seventy-three last October. Grandma and Grandpa had eight younguns, and they was all gone now, not dead, just gone to far-off places to live, though Grandma said they might as well have gone on, no more than she got to see them, just on Christmas mostly. But I could tell she was real happy that her grandboy Leroy Jackson was getting to come and live with us till his pa, Grandma's youngest boy, got home from the war. Once when I asked Grandma why she talked about her boy Tom, Leroy's pa, more than her other young-

uns, she said, "'Cause he's my baby, allus will be—
the first and the last is pure hard to fergit—they has a
way of a-tugging at a body's heartstrings."

Leroy's mom had gone to work in a war plant,
and she didn't want Leroy to be alone, 'cause, like
me, he was an only youngun. I'd never seen Leroy,
but I hated him anyways—hated him just 'cause he
was coming to stay or maybe because Grandma was
his, too. I mean, heck fire, it'd been just me and
Grandma nigh since I could remember, and it was
hard enough to make a living on our twenty-acre hill
farm without having to put up with an uppity city
feller. 'Sides, I reckoned Grandma would like him
better than me. I mean, him being new to her and
all.

I didn't dare tell Grandma how I felt, 'cause she
was a dyed-in-the-wool Christian and didn't hold with
jealousy. I punched the feather bed again and thought
the fact was, there wasn't much Grandma did hold
with 'cept hard work and church-going. I sort of
grinned to myself and thought maybe Leroy wouldn't
stay, poor as the farm was and all. Fact of the matter,
we didn't get out much. About the only reason me
and Grandma knew there was a war on was hearing
war talk at church. We didn't have a radio for news

'cause Grandma said batteries were too dear for us to buy.

I dreaded sleeping with Leroy, too, 'cause we just had two bedrooms, a living room, and a kitchen. Our beds were iron bedsteads, and there were nails to hang extra clothes on. The living room had an old rock fireplace Grandpa had built and some cane rockers he made from river-bottom cane. He'd made the oak table and benches in the kitchen, too, and the washstand by the back door. Grandma said Grandpa had brought the big black cast-iron cookstove from Little Rock on a wagon when they were first wed. The braided rugs on the floor had belonged to Grandma's ma, and our curtains were made from feed sacks Grandma had dyed blue and red.

When I said I wished we had more stuff, Grandma would say, "Spud, a body ken jest wear one pair of drawers at a time, boy." I gave a deep sigh. Me and Grandma had lived all winter on corn bread, pinto beans and potatoes and what milk old Belle, our cow, seen fit to give.

I wished I could sleep. But I felt hungry, for the house still smelled of the cinnamon and brown sugar Grandma had used to make fried apple pies for Leroy. Being hungry wasn't new to me—seemed I was that way ten minutes after I'd eat anyhow. Once I feared I had a tapeworm, but Grandma just laughed and said hunger was the way of growing boys.

I heard Grandma's corn shuck mattress rustling and knowed she was having a hard time sleeping, too, but I bet it was 'cause of the new preacher coming. He was from a far-off place called Russia, a place not even in America, let alone Arkansas. Anyway, he was a preaching man, and folks was a-building a brush arbor not far from Jud Treese's pond. Grandma said some of the folks would be sniffing around him like he was a strange dog. Then, with a sort of worried sigh, she said, "Boy, don't ever judge a hen till ye see how many eggs she ken lay. That's what yore Grandpa used to say." According to Grandma, Grandpa said a lot of things, but I recall him as a real quiet man. 'Course I knowed that was just Grandma's way of saying wait till she seen whether the new preaching man was for himself or God.

I heard Thunder, our old mule, kick his stall in the barn, and someplace far off an owl hooted. And I heard no more till Grandma's voice cracked the wall of sleep around me. "Spud! Spud, git yore chores, boy. Yore cousin is goin' t' be heer afore ye kin spit."

⟨ 10 ⟩

CHAPTER
TWO

I knowed before I seen Leroy I'd have to whip him, and there wasn't a doubt in my mind that I could, for hard work had turned me into a lot of Grandma's whang leather, and hard winters had kept just the muscles and melted off any extra fat. 'Sides, Leroy was a city boy, and any fool knowed a city boy was sissified. 'Course I didn't know it for sure 'fore I got outa bed at Grandma's call 'cause I hadn't seen him yet.

I slipped outa bed into my overalls, thinking it'd

be the last time my bed was mine for a long spell. I stopped at the washstand and cracked the ice to douse my face and slick my hair back, noting that Grandma was shoving a pan of biscuits in the oven and also noting she was wearing one of her good flour sack dresses. "Showin' off fer Leroy," I muttered under my breath.

"Eh? What er ye sayin', boy?" Grandma asked, turning her mop of cotton candy hair my way.

"Jest sayin' I'd hurry with the chores," I answered, stepping out the back door, shivering as the first blast of December wind hit me.

Grandma had already fed Belle and milked her, 'cause Grandma seemed to fear men and boys were never quite clean enough to do the milking. A half dozen barn cats were lapping warm milk from a tin pan. I climbed the ladder to the barn loft and pitched hay to the mule and cow and mixed a bucket of bran to slop the hog. I fed the chickens corn and opened the barn stall doors so Belle and Thunder could go out to pasture.

The old black snake that Grandma had made a pet of slid out of a hole in the side of the cellar where she lived in winter, making me jump 'cause I was never quite sure if it was old Hermie or one of her kinfolks ready to bite the dickens out of me.

Grandma could, and did, make pets out of 'most anything. A body could pat old Hermie on the head like a dog, or she'd crawl on your shoulder and curl up and snooze while you carried her around. But sometimes Hermie got in the hens' nests and swallowed the eggs; then Grandma got mad and chased her with the broom.

I figured it'd be another hour before the mail car brought Leroy to our place, so I went to the house to eat. Grandma hopped around the kitchen like a bird, just stopping to peck at her plate now and then. She was putting beans on to cook for noon dinner.

"Ye swipe that gravy off yer plate, boy, an' get yore jacket. Let's git a-goin'," she said, jamming Grandpa's hat down on her head.

"I allus thought Grandpa said, 'Haste makes waste," I sniggered.

Grandma snapped, "He allus said smart-mouthed younguns needed peach-treeing—real often, too."

"We got us an hour, Grandma," I protested, wanting another biscuit.

"Not time. Not time we walked t' the mailbox in the snow. 'Sides, Abe Marshall is jest as liable t' be early as late with the mail. An' we don't wont Leroy settin' side the road not knowin' which way t' go an' a-freezin' stiff as a board.''

It wouldn't've bothered me at all if Leroy sat beside the road till doomsday and froze, I thought darkly, but didn't dare say it out loud. Staring back regretfully at the still-warm biscuits, I let Grandma pull me out the door.

We walked down the narrow dirt road, sniffing the sharp air. The smell of pine and cedar filled the air, and I eye-picked a Christmas tree for us. Grandma looked at me with a crinkling smile in her eyes and said, ''The Lord done made it plumb pretty, didn't He, boy?''

I nodded, knowing she meant the woods with snow clinging to the branches, and a rabbit that hopped across our path, stopping to wiggle his nose at us. ''I bet he's a-cussin' us, Grandma,'' I said, looking back at the rabbit.

''I reckon he don't like folks a-messin' with his mornin' routine,'' Grandma said like she knowed exactly what the rabbit was thinking.

When we got to the Treese pond and seen the half-built brush arbor, Grandma's lips thinned to a narrow line, and she stopped to stare at the rows of logs that people would sit on and the four corner posts that

⟨14⟩

menfolks would use to make a cover over the logs in case of more snow. But the sides would be left open. There was a large stump in front of the rows of logs that would be used for a pulpit, and it was big enough to set a lantern and a Bible on. In the daylight it looked real peaceful in the little open glen, with the pond, a little behind, a wide round sheet of ice.

The arbor was surrounded by thick-growing trees: persimmon, pine, cedar, oak, black gum, and hickory nut. There was black walnut and sassafras, too. Wild grape vines grew up some of the trees, and old oaks had moss-covered sides. Grandma gave a deep sigh and said, "Ye know, Spud, we jest might come t' that fereign feller's meetin' one of these heer nights. I got me a hankerin' t' heer what he has t' say fer hisself. 'Sides, I ain't never heard no fer-off folks preach afore, though I reckon, boy, all folks is the same. The good Lord jest give us different hides, sorta."

"Well, it's shore He done give ye rawhide leather, Grandma," I laughed.

And she laughed back, saying, "Well, come on. Let's meet that grandboy o' mine."

The happiness in her voice took the fun all out of me, and I stomped gloomily along in my old worn

brogans. I was plenty old enough to know I was being
a baby for not wanting to share Grandma, and knowed
really we couldn't get new shoes just to show off with.
But I couldn't seem to help feeling the way I did. I
mean, iffen any of Grandma's younguns really cared
for her, it seemed to me they'd come to see her a long
time ago. I mean, real often, not just Christmases.

I didn't tell Grandma what I thought because she'd
just say they had families, jobs, and such to take care
of. Grandma never talked about her younguns a whole
lot, and she never talked about my ma atall. Truth to
tell, I hardly ever thought about Ma either. When I
was littler, I used to wonder when she was coming
home to see me, but as I got older I didn't think on
it any more.

We came out on the dirt road by our mailbox, and
Grandma's breath sent little white puffy clouds across
her face. I leaned against the mailbox, thinking maybe
Grandma had never heard a preacher from a far-off
place preach before, and I'd for sure never seen a
person from Detroit, the place where Leroy was coming from. Leastways I could say my cousin's name, I
thought. But the strange preacher was sure beyond
my tongue. Granny Treat said his name was something like Ivor Baldenshick. But nobody could say it

for sure, so everybody would just call him preacher or brother. I mean, our hillfolks was real polite, and they'd not never let him know they couldn't say his name. Truth to tell, I sort of looked forward to hearing one of his meetings, 'cause it wasn't every day new folks came to our hills.

I heard the sputter and clang of Abe Marshall's old truck that he carried the mail on, and stood up stiff as a dog pointing quail, feeling my belly go all empty. When we could see the smoke cloud that the old truck raised, Grandma stood up, sort of hopping from one foot to the other, smoothing her dress down and trying to push her mop of hair up under Grandpa's hat. The old truck came to a sudden stop, throwing snow about. I heard Abe say something to Grandma, but I just had eyes for the boy stepping down from the cab of the truck.

He was my age, but that's where all we had in common stopped. His hair was coal black, parted in the middle and slicked with grease or something, flat to his head. His eyes were blue like Grandma's, and he was dressed grander than anybody I'd ever seen. He had on the kind of britches I'd just seen preachers wear before, and a store-bought shirt, and his shoes were not just black, but a real shiny black. And what made my eyes pop nigh out of my head was a pack of store-bought cigarettes in his shirt pocket in plain sight.

Grandma ran toward him, saying, "My, my, yer jest like Tom. Yer jest like my boy all over again."

I turned away, feeling my whole insides turn pure green. Oh, how I wished my bib overalls would turn into store-bought clothes, and the old brogans on my feet into shiny black shoes. And I'd dearly love to carry a pack of store cigarettes in my shirt pocket like a man grown. But if Grandma ever caught me smoking the wild rabbit tobacco that grew around our place, she would bust my britches with the razor strop Grandpa had used before he'd gone on. That strop was still hanging on the nail. I straightened the old sheepskin jacket of Grandpa's that I was wearing and tried to hand-comb my straw-colored hair. I was wishing I had Grandma's blue eyes 'stead of green ones like an old tomcat.

I didn't come to myself till a cool flat voice said, "Can't ya hear, hick?"

I turned my head to meet the cold smile of my cousin, and he said, soft and mean, "I mean you, rube. Come and carry those suitcases."

I looked at Grandma. Her face was glowing, and

she had not even heard me a-being bad-mouthed by a city stranger. Without a word, I walked over and picked them up.

CHAPTER
THREE

Grandma and Leroy walked ahead, and I staggered along behind them, feeling like my arms were being pulled from their sockets by the two heavy suitcases. I figured Leroy must have more clothes than ten of our hill families, and I thought sourly of the nail on my bedroom wall that held my lone pair of Sunday britches.

Grandma chattered faster than a chipmunk, asking about Leroy's pa and family. It seemed ten miles to the house, and I was surprised my arms were still hanging onto my shoulders. I dropped the suitcases on the porch with a bang and nigh fell down beside them to rest, letting Leroy and Grandma go on into the house.

Rock, our old hound, came snarling around the corner of our house 'cause he knowed good and well the stranger he was supposed to growl at was already in the house. Grandma had named him Rock when we first got him years ago 'cause she said trying to tell him anything was like talking to a rock. Fact of the matter, Grandma said a rock was more apt to learn to act like a dog than Rock was.

The hound was lazy and, truth to tell, sort of afeared of 'most anything that moved. And if something did happen, like a weasel getting to the chicken house, Rock would hide till me or Grandma ran the weasel off, then he'd come growling around like he'd kill anything that came nigh us. In spite of Rock's fault, there was something real likable about him. Maybe it was 'cause he allus acted sort of ashamed of himself.

I patted him on the head, and his big brown eyes sort of slid away from mine. I mean, Rock had a hard time looking anybody or anything in the eye. Rock crawled under the porch, the hiding place he liked best, and I wished I'd crawled under it with him when Grandma called, "Spud! Spud, bring them suitcases in."

I carried the cases into my bedroom and Leroy followed, not saying anything to me. From one of the cases he took a pink dress and gave it to Grandma, saying, "Mom sent this to you."

"Why, 'tis the most beautiful dress I ever did see," Grandma said, her eyes all shiny. I wished fierce I could buy Grandma ten dresses.

"Man, I could use a cup of joe," Leroy said, swaggering into the kitchen, kind of looking around, snorting his nose.

"A cup of joe?" Grandma asked, puzzled.

"You know. Uh, java. Coffee."

"Well, I know what coffee be, boy," Grandma laughed, and went on, "but yer a little young t' be drinkin' it, ain't ye?"

"Oh, no, I'm not, Grandma," Leroy said out the side of his mouth. "I've been drinking coffee for a year or so."

"An' yore ma lets ye?" Grandma asked, sort of shocked.

"Mom works almost day and night in the war plant. I take care of myself," Leroy bragged.

Grandma didn't say nothing else, but I saw her lips tighten a little as she poured coffee for him, and resentment built up in me 'cause Grandma wouldn't ever let me drink coffee. I think then and there I went more 'n a little crazy 'cause I grabbed a cup and swaggered to the stove and poured myself some coffee, and like to have died of shock when it didn't taste like it smelled. But I wouldn't have let on it was my first cup of coffee in my life if it had killed me.

"Man, it's dead, but dead around here," Leroy said, leaning back in his chair and lighting a cigarette. I felt my hair raise, and I cast a slant-eyed look at Grandma. In a flash she plucked the cigarette from Leroy's fingers and raised the stove lid and dumped it in the fire.

In a firm voice that surprised me, she said, "Leroy, I don't hold with younguns smokin' or drinkin' coffee. Milk and cold spring water is plenty good fer growin' boys. Now, Spud, ye an' Leroy heed me and recollect I ain't got no schoolin' fer a-sayin' big words t' folks' understandin'. I know yer sayin' Grandma don't understand young, an' mebbe I have fergot some." Grandma's eyes looked sort of dreamy and far off, her cotton candy hair floating around her head like a soft white cloud.

Then her gaze jerked back to us, and she said gentle-like, "I reckon that young means tastin' the crisp in apples, the drip in the butter, the sweet of the sweet potatoes, and the snap and tang of mustard green."

A little sadly she went on. "'Tis feeling good when the frost nips yore nose an' ears an' the sap raises up under yer skin. Young, 'tis feelin' air clean to yer lungs an' yer feet dancified. I do reckon young is the live in livin', an' ye see, boys, as ye git older an' keep on a-pollutin' yer body with cigarettes an' coffee an' such, it takes a little more sugar fer the sweet 'taters 'cause of yer mouth bein' dulled, an' the air don't quite reach yer lungs, an' yer feet don't feel dancified so much.

"Now, I don't say cigarettes an' coffee will send ye t' hell, 'cause I don't believe that. But I'd bet ol' Becky's feathers it'll git ye t' heaven pretty fast."

"Grandma, you drink coffee," Leroy protested, and Grandma nodded her head.

"'Tis the choice I made when I was wed," she said. "I didn't know it would be a habit, an' nobody told me nay. An' I cain't keep y'all from habits neither, jest tell ye what I learned from a-livin'. But I ken an' will keep ye from cigarettes an' coffee while yer under my roof. Make no mistake about that."

I wasn't, and from looking at Leroy, I could tell he wasn't neither. I had to swallow a lump in my throat, for looking at Grandma's toothless face I wished fierce she could again taste the crisp of an apple. Grandma picked Leroy's coffee up and dumped it out the back door, saying, "Spud, go t' the springhouse an' bring us some cold milk."

I was glad to, for the look on Leroy's face was about to make me laugh. I mean, he looked so red-mad, like he wanted to bust and didn't know which way to bust in. But when I got back with the milk pail I found out, 'cause he was saying real mean to Grandma, "Listen, Grandma, I'm the boss on the street where I live and nobody tells Leroy Jackson what he can drink or smoke. I can drink more beer than any of the gang."

Grandma gasped with shock, for Grandma didn't hold with younguns talking back to older folks atall. I fully expected Grandma to half slap his head off like she'd do me iffen I back-talked her. But she just looked sort of sad and said, "Ye best git ol' clothes on, boy. Yore fancy ones is apt t' git messed up on a farm."

"Oh, I'm not worried about it," Leroy said, look-

⟨ 25 ⟩

ing back down at the table. "There's plenty more where those came from."

He drank milk and told us—or Grandma, 'cause he never looked at me—about his life. Acted like I wasn't there at all. He talked about his pa being gone for a year or more in the Army and bragged of all the money his ma made in the war plant, saying she bought him all the clothes he wanted 'cause she couldn't be with him herself.

Me and Grandma both sat with our mouths open 'cause we'd never in our born days heard of such things. He told about living in an apartment and having electric lights and a toilet in the house and water that a body didn't have to heat and more people on the streets than we had for miles around. He told about street cars, trains, buses, and taxicabs, and Grandma's lips got tighter and tighter the more he bragged. As for me, I figured he lied about half of what he told us.

When he got to bragging about whopping up on the street gang leader, I got up from the table and went to fill the woodbox, 'cause my belly was plumb full of my cousin Leroy Jackson. 'Sides, he didn't seem to know I was alive. When I brought the wood back in, he was looking at the noon dinner Grandma had set on the table like it was slop for the hogs. I slid into my place, thinking it was a right good dinner. I mean, Grandma had fixed extra good 'cause Leroy was coming, making the fried apple pies and all.

Leroy looked surprised when Grandma bowed her head and asked the blessing, but as soon as the amen was said, he asked, "Do you have any bologna and bread, Grandma?" Then growled, "I could use a sandwich."

So could I, I thought, about a dozen of them, but sandwiches on store bread was a treat we only had once a year if then, and mostly at church suppers or when the kinfolks came for Christmas.

Grandma said, still calm, "This is good decent food, boy, an' it will be the only kind ye git heer."

"Then I'll not be stayin' long," Leroy said. He pushed his chair back.

"Ye'll stay till yer ma sends fer ye," Grandma said firmly but very kindly. If I'd have talked like Leroy done, she'd have boxed my ears half off.

I seen Leroy's face getting all red and could see him plain getting ready to bad-mouth Grandma. Jumping up, I grabbed Leroy by the arm. "I got somethin' I wont ye t' see," I said, half dragging him.

Grandma sort of protested, but I kept dragging Leroy. When we was outside the door, with the door shut, Leroy yanked away from me and hissed, "What's so damned important for me to see?"

I hissed right back, "I wont ye t' see how I beat the hell out of a city slicker."

CHAPTER
FOUR

"Where do you want to start?" Leroy asked, then grinned real friendly right in my face. That's when I knowed I'd made a mistake. I mean, I knowed Leroy was gonna wipe up the ground with me. Still, I couldn't let him bad-mouth Grandma.

"Down in the orchard," I said, tiredly pointing down the hill, already knowing I was whipped.

I started walking down the hill and went stiff when Leroy put his arm around me like we was lifelong pals and said, still friendly, "Say, how come you want to beat me up, rube?"

"My name is Spud," I said cool as I could, but inside my voice wanted to break. Truth to tell, I was scared green. "An' the reason I'm gonna pound on ye, Leroy, is 'cause o' the way ye talk t' Grandma," I said out loud.

"Big hero," Leroy sneered. He pushed me away from him. "She's my grandma the same as yours, rube, and I'll talk to her any way I damn well please."

We walked under the bare apple trees and, truth to tell, that's just about the last thing I can remember clear, 'cause Leroy said, "Is this the place?" and before I could finish nodding, he whacked me on the chin with his fist and sent me flying rear over head to bounce off an old scarred apple tree, skidding in the snow. Leroy laughed and said, "You can't be a Blue Devil if you're so easy to whip, hick, and I was the leader of the pack." And he went on talking, dancing around, his breath steaming white as I shook my head and tried to get the snow out of my eyes and ears and get the ground to lay still under my feet.

"Boy, would the boys laugh if they could see me fightin' with my fists," he crowed.

"What in the cat hair do ye fight with?" I asked, staggering to my feet.

"Chains, iron bars."

"Ye mean ye try t' kill each other?" I asked, surprised.

"Well, the others have knives, and once one of the Yellowjackets had a gun."

"Well, all I got is me," I said, lunging at him. From then on it was just me trying to get up and him knocking me back down. I didn't know what else to do, so just kept trying to get up and got flattened for my pains. I felt one lick split my lip and another smash my nose, and after a while my eyes sort of puffed up till I could just see through narrow slits.

Leroy started saying, "You want to quit? You want to give up?" but it seemed I'd sort of got in the habit of being knocked down by then. I remember thinking sometime that from now on, Grandma could flat take up for herself. Then Leroy sort of started begging me to quit standing up, saying, "Aw, come on, Spud. Man, I don't want to kill you. Why don't you stay down? You're whipped. Lay there."

I remember thinking, I'll stand up one more time, then I'll die. I pulled myself up by grabbing the old apple tree and fell straight into Leroy's arms and we both went down. When I came to, Leroy was wiping my face off with a handful of snow, saying, "You might not be the best fighter I've ever seen, Spud, but you're the best stander-upper I ever ran into," and I hung onto him as he half-dragged me to the house. And I knowed somehow, some way I'd get even with my city cousin.

I nigh passed out again when Grandma seen us, 'cause she said, "Ye been a-fightin', Spud Tackett, an' I never thought I'd see the day I was plumb ashamed of a youngun I'd raised. A-fightin' yore blood kin who ain't had time t' know our ways."

I felt shock go through me and figured it was a darn good thing Leroy was holding me up. Lord o' mercy, it looked to me Grandma would've knowed I was fighting to protect her. She didn't give me a chance to protest. "Ye ain't too old t' get yore britches busted, an' I ain't too old t' do it."

I stood up as tall as I could, pulling away from Leroy and peering down at Grandma through half-closed eyes. I said, "I'll go wash up at the well, but I won't be goin' t' the barn, Grandma. Fact o' the matter, I ain't never goin' t' the barn t' git my britches busted no more." I seen Grandma's face go white, but she just stared cold right back at me and sort of nodded, her lips thin.

I went to wash the blood off me and thought there was no way in the world I could win. I mean, I

fought—or leastways got hit a lot—to stick up for
Grandma, only to have her turn on me. And now that
he knowed he could, Leroy would no doubt pound
me good even if the sun went under a cloud, or most
anything he didn't like.

The rest of the day Grandma acted like I wasn't
even there. She just talked to Leroy. But a strange
thing happened. Leroy acted plumb friendly toward
me and called me Spud instead of rube or hick. He
even followed me to the barn when I went to do the
chores, and, truth to tell, I sort of enjoyed him telling
me about his gang.

Then he said, "Ya know, Spud, the way you can
take a beating, you'd do good in a gang."

"Ye mean while folks was a-beatin' me t' death
the rest could git away."

Leroy laughed and helped to toss the hay to Belle
and Thunder. Leroy's eyes popped when I took hold
of Belle's tits to squirt some milk in the cat bowls.
"Hey, man, that's not very polite," he protested, and
I grinned.

"If you can figger out a better way to get the milk
out, I'll be the politest cow milker around."

"Is that a jackass or what?" Leroy asked, pointing
to old Thunder.

⟨33⟩

"Mostly a what." I laughed, making my split lip sting. "He's a mule, and I reckon mules is jest fer working, 'cause he shore don't take kindly to being rode."

Grandma still wasn't talking to me at supper, but I didn't care 'cause I didn't feel like talking noways. My mouth was sore. My face ached and throbbed. I went to bed at first dark.

My dreading sharing a bed was a waste of time, 'cause I never knowed when Leroy came to bed. Next morning Leroy tried lighting a cigarette again, and again Grandma plucked it out of his hand and burned it in the cookstove.

I could tell Leroy was mad, and a little puzzled, too. I mean, even he knew a body couldn't go around punching their grandma. I'm not real sure when me and Leroy sort of started being friends, but I think it was when old Hermie hung herself around Leroy's neck and I had to run him down to get her off him. He'd been sitting on the cellar steps waiting for me to finish the chores, and the snake had sneaked up on him.

I heard a scream and looked up to see Leroy flying across the barn lot, old Hermie hanging around his neck like a dirty rope. Leroy's hair wasn't flat no more, and his face looked pure green.

"Stop!" I called.

Leroy yelled, "Can't! Snake's got me!"

"Quit yer running and I'll pull her off." But all I could hear from Leroy was "Can't," so I took after him and run him almost to the pond, slipping and sliding in the snow. Nigh the edge I brought him down with a flying tackle and sit on him while I unwound old Hermie from around his neck. I said, "This old snake won't hurt ye."

Leroy said nothin', just leaned over a snowbank and puked. And from that day on, he helped me with the chores and I helped him sneak his cigarettes behind the barn till his pack ran out.

I was glad Grandma didn't know how much she caused Leroy to sin. I mean, he cussed under his breath all the way to church. 'Sides, he hadn't wanted to go to church nohow. Said at home he never went to church. Said he spent the day with his gang while his ma slept on her only day off.

Grandma strode on ahead of us, her dress tail swinging and Grandpa's hat pushing her hair down. She wore the new pink dress Leroy brought her. "Ye know yore Grandpa allus said folks ought to go to church on Sunday to get a refill of God's spirit, jest like fillin' yore car with gas," Grandma called back over her shoulder. Me and Leroy acted like we didn't hear, for fear Grandma would keep telling us more stuff Grandpa said. Fact of the matter, Grandpa didn't seem dead at all.

Leroy looked around at the woods and snow and up at the blue sky, the sun now shining, and said, "Ya know, Spud, in some ways this is not a bad place."

"Ye'll like it even better when I teach ye how t' hunt an' fish in the spring," I said, feeling proud of our Arkansas hills.

Then Leroy cut his eyes around and said, "Spud, did ya see how that ol' granny of ours wrung them chickens' heads off?"

I laughed and said, "Well, I've seen her do it 'most ever' Sunday of my life. Time we git home they'll be good eatin' the way Grandma bakes 'em slow in the Dutch oven."

"I like chicken as good as anyone," Leroy said, "but I don't know about killing things like that. Grandma just picked them up and wrung their heads off." Then he shook his own head like he still couldn't believe it.

"Leroy, the only way we got t' eat chicken is a-killin' them. How did ye git meat in Detroit?"

"From the store," Leroy said.

"Well, heer the store is jest fer coffee an' flour an' sech. The rest o' the stuff ye have t' raise or hunt."

"Well, I have a feeling that Grandma could wring our necks as easy as she did the chickens if we don't do to suit her," Leroy said. Then he laughed. "Boy, I bet she'd make a mean Blue Devil."

I laughed, too, then said, "Grandma would have yer whole gang a-goin' t' prayer meetin' an' prayin' fer each other 'fore ye could pull that long-bladed knife yer carryin'."

Before Leroy could say anything else, Grandma called, "Ye boys shake a leg now." So we hurried to catch up with her. When we passed the brush arbor by the pond, me and Grandma both stared in surprise 'cause leastways half the brush arbor was finished and I figured it wouldn't be long before the new preacher came. And I might have given it more thought if I'd known he was going to bust our hill lives wide open.

CHAPTER
FIVE

Old Brother Rose was waiting on the schoolhouse steps to welcome his congregation, which was mighty few this Sunday. His old bald head was shining in the sun. I shook hands with him, but couldn't hardly look at him, for his eyes had a sort of puzzled hurt look as he stared down the road like he hoped he'd see other folks coming 'fore long.

Grandma introduced Leroy to him and said kindly, "They ain't nobody else a-comin', Brother Rose, 'cause they's all a-waitin' fer the new preacher t' come."

Leroy was sort of uneasy 'cause of not being in church before, so I sat on the back bench with him. The one-room school was emptier than I'd ever seen it on a Sunday. There was mostly old granny women, Abe Marshall and his bunch, and younguns, 'cause of the menfolks going to war.

Leroy looked surprised at the clear sweetness of Grandma's voice as it raised in an old hymn she loved. Then I remembered, he didn't know Grandma the way I did. After the song service Brother Rose spoke gently about straying sheep, and I reckon he was thinking of the folks missing from his flock. And he told how Jesus loved all his people, even the strayed ones. Leroy squirmed, restless, and, truth to tell, I got a mite tired of sitting myself, though I was more used to it than he was.

After church we hurried home for the big heavy meal we always had on Sundays. Me and Leroy helped Grandma set the table, and I ran to the cellar for the blue bowl of fresh churned butter and a jar of pear preserves Grandma had canned the year before. Grandma made buttermilk biscuits and smashed-up fluffy potatoes to go with the roast chickens. Then she made yellow gravy from the chicken broth to pour over the potatoes.

I could tell by the way Leroy dug into the food that

he'd forgotten all about store bread and bologna. He didn't gripe about helping clean up the dishes like he usually did, neither. Truth to tell, I reckon he was nigh afraid not to mind Grandma, just as I was.

I reckon she had forgotten about me and Leroy's fight 'cause she hadn't said nothing else about it. Grandma went to sit in her rocker, and I took Leroy down to the orchard to show him how to smoke rabbit tobacco. I showed him how to pick the silver-gray leaves off the low-growing plants and how to crumble them up in bits of brown paper, though the leaves was 'most frozen. 'Course, a body allus coughed and choked when they took their first drag or two. Finally we stood with our backs leaning against the apple tree, and the sun felt good. The whole hills were sort of dozing in the sun like Grandma in her rocker. Water dripped slowly from the icicles on the house and cellar.

Leroy said lazily, "How come Grandma's so against people smoking in the house?"

"Grandma is against folks smoking anyplace," I said. "She says iffen the Lord made a body t' smoke, it'd be comin' out their ears."

Leroy laughed and so did I. Then he said, serious, "I suppose the Lord didn't care if we smoke, else tobacco wouldn't grow. Do you think so, Spud?''

"Well, t' tell the truth, Leroy, I don't know what the Lord thinks. I mean—well, they's all sorts o' things growin' that a body don't smoke or eat either, an' some folks don't even know what it is. No, sir, Leroy, I don't have me no idea what the good Lord 'spects us t' do.''

"Do you feel bad about smoking, Spud?''

I wanted to brag and say no, but he was looking at me so solemn I told the truth. "Well, I sorta feel bad—fact, I feel bad doin' most anythin' Grandma says is wrong. An' truth t' tell, tobacco sorta makes me sick. But it jest seems smokin' is somethin' a boy ort t' do. Fact, I don't know many menfolks who don't smoke.''

"My dad don't smoke. Least he didn't when he went into the army,'' Leroy said then, sounding bitter.

"Are you mad at yore pa, Leroy?'' I asked.

"No,'' he said, fast, "I mean not real mad, but it seems like he could have waited longer to join the army, like the other men—I mean until he was called. Man, him being gone is hard on Mom. My dad went almost a year before the other men,'' Leroy said, half proud and half mad.

"You really don't care, do you?" I asked.

Leroy just looked at me and laughed. "Well, I sure the hell don't care for rabbit tobacco, Spud," he said, putting the cigarette out. "Let's leave it to the rabbits."

I laughed and put mine out, too.

"You want to teach me how to hunt or fish now, Spud?"

"Cain't today," I said, getting up. "Grandma don't hold with doing such on the Lord's day. 'Sides, in winter all ye ken hunt is rabbits."

"Is there much Grandma don't hold with?" Leroy said, and we both laughed. I mean, sort of men's laugh about womenfolks, not a bad-feeling laugh.

We wandered down through the orchard to our pond. "Have you ever been with a girl, Spud?" Leroy asked.

I felt my ears turn red and said sort of gruff, "Yep," but I knowed I wasn't meaning what he did.

"Are there any around here that fool around?"

Then, right then, I knowed how I was going to get even with Leroy Jackson, and I tried hard to keep from grinning. "A few," I said, trying to think of one. Then, before he could ask more, I said real fast, "Tessie Martin is easy. Ye'll meet her in school. She kisses all the boys. Have ye been with a gal, Leroy?''

''Umm, well, umm, well, I stole a girl from one of the Outlaws gang once.''

''What happened?'' I asked, and felt my voice crack.

''He got her back, but not before I'd kissed her,'' Leroy said boastfully, and looking at him close I could tell he was lying same as me, so I said, laughing, ''Grandma don't hold with girl-foolin' till a boy's wed, neither.'' Then I said, ''Maybe Grandma will let me show ye how t' rabbit hunt, long as we don't really hunt today.''

We went to the kitchen, where Grandma was cooking, and Leroy said, ''Grandma, can Spud show me how to rabbit hunt? We won't really do it.''

''Well, I cain't see no harm in him a-showin','' Grandma said slowly, then turned to me. ''Ye go feed Rock 'fore ye leave this house,'' Grandma snapped, sharp-like.

''I'll feed him when I git back,'' I said sullenly. I was wanting to feel the .22 in my hands.

''Ye'll do it right now, Spud Tackett,'' Grandma said, her hands on her hips and Grandpa's hat falling over one eye. I could tell she was spitting mad when she said, ''Jest how would ye like it iffen I jest fed

ye when I felt like it? Ye don't jest feed a dog or any
other animal when ye feel like it. They got feelin's
too. They hurt an' git hungry an' no tellin' what else.
So ye give that dog some clean water, too.''

I hurried out the door, Grandma following me to
the porch. I slopped Rock's food in his pan, most of
it going in the snow and dirt, but if Rock minded he
never let on, just lapped it up. Grandma's eyes were
blazing at me, and I was sort of scared, but she just
sort of sputtered, ''Ye jest wait, Spud Tackett. Ye
jest wait.''

I flew around the house and drew up water from
the well and hurriedly poured it in Rock's bowl, then
ran out the gate to where Leroy waited.

We walked for miles, me showing Leroy how to
track rabbits in the snow and how to follow them to
hollow logs and such. After hours in the snow we
could hardly wait to get home. We were tired and half
froze. We could smell the beans and hot corn bread
at the gate, and 'most ran in the kitchen and slid into
the benches, nigh drooling till Grandma said grace.

Before I could take a bite out of my heaping plate,
Grandma said, ''Hold on, Spud,'' and snatched my
plate from under my open mouth. ''Follow me,'' she
said grimly, and, puzzled, I followed her out on the

porch and down the steps. And my mouth opened even farther when she dumped my plate in Rock's dish, running it over the side into the dirt and gravel. Then in a sad voice she said, "I'm right sure ye won't mind havin' t' lick yore food from between the rocks. As yore grandpa used t' say, a little dirt never hurt nobody."

I saw red and stared pure hate at the little woman staring back at me so sad, and since a body didn't hit grandmas, no matter how riling they be, I let out a mad squall and flew around the house to the barn. Kicking and hitting the side of the barn, I cussed blue, then cussed some words I didn't know I knew, and pure tears of shame dripped from my face. My grandma had shamed me afore Leroy.

A feeling came that I might have brought it on myself, but I didn't want to think on it. I lay back on the hay of a barn stall we used for feed storage and tried to stop crying. And it was Rock who came, shifty-eyed, to tenderly lick my hand like he was sorry and shamed, too. Quiet came over me, and I patted his head, and a worse shame filled me for the thought of all the times I'd dumped Rock's food in the dirt and the times I'd let his water scum over.

But still, I'd rather Grandma beat me than do what

she done. I didn't want to leave the barn. I wanted to stay there forever. I didn't want to face Grandma and Leroy, and decided bitterly that maybe me and Rock would go off in the woods to live together.

I didn't know Leroy was around till suddenly he said, "Man, oh, man, that Grandma is the meanest little lady I have ever seen," and he whistled through his teeth.

I was shocked when a sort of pride came up in me and I said, "Ye ken bet yore britches on it."

Leroy looked sort of proud, too, and said, "I wish I could have had her on our side when the Black Raiders tried to wipe out the Blue Devils." Then suddenly we were grinning at each other, and the shame faded out of me.

CHAPTER
SIX

Leroy snickered all the way to school. He thought it was funny to attend school in the church house. I tried to tell him it was a school, just used for church on Sundays and Wednesday night prayer meetings and for socials like box suppers and pie suppers. Fact of the matter, when I got to talking about it, it seemed less like a school than ever, but it was mine and I didn't want it bad-mouthed.

Another fact was that I wasn't so sure now that I really liked Leroy. I mean, I was just beginning to.

⟨47⟩

Then I saw him drag his new britches out of his suit-
case and put on his shiny shoes. I tried to slick my
hair down the way he did, but it kept popping up in
rooster tails. I even tried carrying Grandma's short
butcher knife; though it was a sad sight compared to
the one Leroy had. Anyway, it fell through a hole in
my pocket and I gave up. 'Sides, I never needed anything but my pocketknife nohow.

The only thing I had to keep me going was knowing that soon I was going to get even for the whipping
Leroy gave me the day he came. But, truth to tell, in
a way I sort of felt sorry for him.

We kicked caked snow from our shoes and eased
into the schoolhouse and sat on the benches in back
of our desks. The teacher's desk had taken the place
of Brother Rose's pulpit that now stood in a corner
nigh the blackboard.

One thing, Leroy quit snickering when he got a
look at Miz Mise, our teacher. Truth to tell, she was
enough to make anybody stop grinning. Sour, she was,
sour and time-dried, thin-lipped and still-eyed, allus
ready to thump a body cross-eyed with her ruler or
make you stand in front of the blackboard with your
nose in a ring till your ears fell off. And the shame
of it was ever there, 'cause there were allus some

smart alecks ready to snicker at your defenseless back.

It was said that Miz Mise had been disappointed in love, but I figured the one who disappointed her would have been more disappointed had they wed.

There were about fifteen of us in the one-room school—first to eighth grade. We all made good grades for the simple reason we had to or face Miz Mise, and not only her, our folks. After the teacher pinned our ears back, she'd go to our houses and tell our folks how no good we were, and our folks would bust our britches good, 'cause in our hills the teachers were always right, no matter what. And it nigh gave a body heart failure to hear her old car chugging up to your house after school of an evening or on Saturdays.

Being an eighth grader, I suspected Miz Mise made up what she didn't know for sure, because we only had three orange crates of books, and that mostly spelling, history, arithmetic, and geography. We had one health book that told a body what to eat and such. I sort of thought it was dumb, I mean dumb for us, 'cause it just made a body hungry for what they didn't have. Still, it was good to have somebody's word 'sides Grandma's that you ought to brush your teeth a lot.

I looked around and saw Gilbert Massey pass a note

to Maisey June Harness. They were in seventh grade and sweet on each other. All the boys wore old patched overalls like me, and the girls wore flower-print flour sack dresses in blue or pink, 'cept Tessie Martin. She wore overalls like a boy, and her copper-brown hair was braided so tight it pulled her pansy-brown eyes to a slant, and she had a pug nose with freckles across it. Her cheeks looked like they had trapped the pink of the wild summer roses to hold for winter.

I thought she was the best thing ever to look at, and I reckon Leroy did too 'cause he kept staring at her through our class.

At first recess he said, "That the easy one, Spud?"

I nodded yes, feeling bad and good at the same time.

All the students were staring at Leroy like he was a strange dog in the pack, and the boys acted like they weren't looking, and the girls giggled crazy like girls do. Some of the little kids got in a snowball fight, and out of the corner of my eye I saw Leroy follow Tessie around the end of the schoolhouse. All our breaths sent tiny puffy clouds over the schoolyard, and my ears seemed to grow, I was listening so hard.

Then I heard it, Leroy's voice. "Ow, don't! Don't! Stop that!"

A wide grin split my face, and even the little kids stopped flinging snowballs to listen to Leroy's beller. "Stop it, dammit! Girls are not supposed to do that. Owww! Turn me loose. Quit it. Ouch!" Then Leroy came tearing around the schoolhouse, skidding to a stop where I stood. One eye was swelling shut, and a trickle of blood came from his nostril. His bottom lip was split, and he hopped on one leg, and I could 'most feel his shin aching. He grabbed me and shook my hair about out, hissing, "You said she was easy. You said she was easy!"

"I didn't say easy to what," I snapped, and he turned me loose as the bell rang.

When the schoolroom quieted, Miz Mise peered steelily at Leroy, saying, "Ye have been fightin', Leroy?"

I saw Leroy gulp and turn red, and I knowed he was sort of confused, for after all, he hadn't been fighting. He'd just been standing letting a girl beat the dickens out of him. Figuring he'd taken all I wanted him to in the first place, I stood up on trembling legs and croaked, "Me an' Leroy was a-wrestlin' in the snow, Miz Mise, an' his face sorta hit a rock under it."

Miz Mise stared at me so long I could feel my gizzard creeping up my throat to choke me to death. Then it fell with a gulp when she said as kind as she ever could, "Well, take your cousin to the pump house and wash the blood from his face."

With a heartfelt, "Yes, ma'am," I grabbed Leroy and nigh dragged him from the school. Then he made me feel lower than a snake by saying, "Hey, thanks, man. You're all right, Spud," as I swiped the blood off him. Then his eyes turned mean and he said, "If you ever breathe a word about a girl whipping the leader of the Blue Devils, I'll kill you dead, Spud Tackett."

"I was just about to send Detroit a telegram," I said sarcastically, but my insides shook at the look in his eye.

The rest of the day Tessie stared at Leroy like she plumb admired him, making him squirm. He acted like he was trying not to look at Tessie, but his eyes kept sliding her way, and his face was red.

Miz Mise said, "Leroy, will you please stand and give us our history lesson for today?" Leroy's Adam's apple jumped nine to the dozen, and his voice sounded dry as he stood and said, "It's about the Civil War and the South was whipped by the North and the slaves set free"—Leroy's voice got faster and faster— "and the North took over the South's government."

Tessie shot to her feet, yelling, "It ain't true, Leroy Jackson! We ain't never been whipped, and we ain't never gonna be! Yore jest a dumb ol' northern boy, Leroy, an' the South whipped up on the Yankees jest like I done on ye!"

I didn't think Leroy's face could get any redder, but it did, 'cause all the school was snickering at him.

Miz Mise said, "That's enough, Tessie," and "You can sit down, Leroy."

Leroy sort of fell down in his seat and acted like he was studying hard the rest of the day.

When we got home, Leroy told Grandma he got hit in the eye with a hard snowball. Grandma looked skeptically at us both, but only said, "Ye ready fer yer supper? The new preacher's done come, an' I thought after supper we'd go heer what all the folks are talkin' about."

CHAPTER
SEVEN

People stirred restlessly, and I could feel a sort of excitement that made my hair want to rise. I stared around me and saw some of the Treeses and Wattses, a Tilley or two, and the Rosages and Morrises and other folks I couldn't make out in the shadows. A baby whimpered now and then, and once in a while a big boy and girl would snicker, nervous-like.

Just when it seemed to me something was going to burst, old Frank Satterfield rose up beside the stump pulpit with his fiddle, and Billy Mise, the teacher's brother, joined him with his banjo. They tore into a foot-stomping tune of "I'll Fly Away, O Glory" and other church songs that sort of didn't sound like church songs, but folks were stomping their feet and clapping their hands. My own feet were tapping time, but when I stole a look at Grandma, her face was stern and set.

Leroy was just looking scared and sort of leaning on Grandma. I nigh climbed a tree myself when old Granny Treat jumped up shouting, "Glory, Glory!" and stuff.

When the music and singing stopped, there was dead quiet—a quiet that sort of made a body sick. Maybe like sort of waiting for a storm to hit. And hit it did, but in the form of a man, a huge man who seemed to leap out of the darkness of the forest behind the stump pulpit. A sort of moan went up through the people, and hearing Grandma suck in a long hissing breath, fear shot through me. Even before the stranger spoke.

He was a big man, tall and fair, his hair almost silver in the firelight, and his eyes were a clear color. His face was reddish, and his teeth showed white when he smiled. And that's all he done—smile, I mean— till folks stopped moving and got so quiet you could hear the trees crackling in the cold.

⟨55⟩

Just when I thought the preacher wasn't going to say nothing at all, he screamed, "You are all going to hell!"

Me and Leroy both tried to jump off the log, but Grandma latched onto us and held us down. Most of the folks at the meeting cried out in protest, but his deep voice beat them quiet, and he yelled, "Yes! Ye are goin' t' hell t' be roasted on the pitchfork o' the devil, and ye'll scream fer mercy, but there'll be none."

The picture of me turning on a pitchfork made my hair stand up, and for the first time in my life I wanted to be saved bad. Fact of the matter, saved was all I wanted to be in the whole world. I'd heard about hell before, I mean sort of knowed it was there. But I didn't think on it much—maybe I figgered Grandma would get me outa it some way. The new preacher screaming about it made it seem more real, like it was just waitin' to grab me. And truth to tell, iffen there was anyplace I didn't want to go, it was hell.

The preacher started saying, "Ye ain't seen no hell till ye seen war! War on yore very porch, seen yore younguns killed before yore eyes and things done to yore womenfolk that I can't speak on 'cause it would be so bad. Ever' man here would grab his gun and go after them yellow devils. Why, most of our men that went over to the war has already been killed. Nobody ain't telling ye that, 'cause they's afeared the rest of ye will run fer the hills—like ye should.''

I glanced at Leroy. He was glaring at the preacher with a funny look on his face, but it shore wasn't a laughing funny look.

"And there is only one way to be saved from the flames of hell," the preacher yelled on, "and that's to follow me!''

I remember thinking it strange that a fereign feller talked like us, but then I forgot it 'cause, Lord o' mercy, he was giving us a way to escape hell.

"Yes, follow me," he yelled in a voice that rang with sincerity. "I was sent by the Lord Almighty from a land thousands and thousands of miles across the sea t' tell an' show ye the way, the way t' be released from yer hell-bound ways. An' we'll trod the path t' Glory.''

"Trod the path! Glory, Glory!'' folks shouted.

And he again quieted them. Dropping his voice to a sound so gentle a body could 'most hear the angels sing, he said, "Follow me, my chil'en. Follow me as ye know in yer heart Jesus is askin' ye t' do.'' Then, raising his voice, he screamed, "I'm an angel o' the

Lord, sent t' ye t' lead ye t' the promised land! Brothers and sisters, will ye follow me?"

I stared at the preacher standing quiet, waiting for the folks to say something. His eyes were wide and red-looking with the fire reflected in them, his short hair glowed like little strings of silver wire, and his mouth was open, showing teeth white and sharp-looking. He looked like a mad dog I'd seen once when the dog days of summer were upon us, but I shook the feeling off 'cause I figgered the Lord wouldn't send no mad folk to preach. I mean I'd never heard of a mad preacher before, and if there was such a thing shorely Grandma would have said.

Then I could hardly think at all, 'cause folks started screaming back, "Yes, brother, show us the way."

"Come t' the mourners' bench," he yelled, "an' make yer peace with God, then later I'll tell ye what the Lord would have ye do."

There was a stampede toward the stump where a log had been laid for the mourners' bench, and me and Leroy tried to go, but Grandma grabbed us both by the arm and hissed, "C'mon, boys, we're goin' home."

"But, Grandma, I want to be saved from hell," Leroy sobbed. And I said, "Let me go, Grandma, I don't wont t' be toasted on no pitchfork.''

"Now, now,'' Grandma said, soothing, like taming wild things. "Ye jest both come on home. Ain't nobody gonna burn ye on no pitchforks.''

Me and Leroy both stared longingly at the folks kneeling and moaning around the log in the firelight, but Grandma tugged and pulled us toward the house.

We were still sort of shivering when Grandma got us in the house and lit the lamp. Being in a place I knowed all my life helped me some, and even Leroy lost some of his wild-eyed look.

"Sit at the table,'' Grandma said, stirring up the fire and putting the coffee on to heat. "Yore grandpa used to say they's times when a cup of coffee is like medicine.'' And with that, she put me and Leroy a cup on the table, too, making our eyes pop.

I reckon there's something about stark fear that makes a body sort of ashamed, 'cause it was hard for me to look Grandma, or Leroy either, in the eye.

Grandma poured us the coffee and sat down, saying, "Now, boys, we're gonna do us some talkin'.''

It was quiet for a spell, then I burst out, "Grandma, how come you wouldn't let us get saved?''

"Boy, I'd be the first t' wont my flesh an' blood saved iffen ye was a-gettin' saved 'cause ye truly loved the Lord an' wonted t' be with Him an' do His will. An' iffen ye was doin' it with understandin' 'stead o' bein' half scared t' death an' not really knowin' what ye was a-doin'.''

"But, Grandma, that preacher was sent. I mean, he's an angel from the Lord sent to save us," Leroy protested.

Grandma sort of grinned and said dryly, "Well, Leroy, I do sorta have my doubts on the Lord a-havin' sent an angel from thousands and thousands o' miles across the sea t' us folks heer in the Arkansas hills.''

"But how do ye know he ain't no angel from God, Grandma?" I asked.

"Well, for one thing, iffen he was, he'd've asked folks t' follow God, not hisself. An' next, I know what I know 'cause I've been a child of God for too many years t' recollect. An' I been all them years a-readin' the Bible, an' He tells us plain as day t' be on the lookout fer wolves dressed up like sheep.

"Now, when 'tis time, when ye are real sure ye know what yer doin', ye come t' me or Brother Rose or, fer that matter, ye ken git saved plumb by yerselves. I mean, jest ye an' God," Grandma said. She sipped her coffee.

"How does a person get saved, Grandma?" Leroy asked.

"Well, ye jest tell God yer right sorry fer yer sinful ways an' ask Him t' save yer soul, an' iffen ye believe it, He will."

"Ye mean it's that easy?" I asked.

"Well, that's what plumb fools some folks," Grandma said. "Ye know, they's folks who's real smart in the ways o' the world, so smart they think gettin' saved is somethin' they have t' study a lot t' find out about.

"And sometimes I do wonder iffen it ain't us old folks that keeps other folks from believin'," Grandma said sadly. "I mean, we teach little younguns t' believe in God an' Santa Claus an' good fairies an' sech, an' when they git bigger we say, 'They ain't really no Santa Claus an' they ain't really no fairies', an' I reckon some of them think we was lyin' about God, too.

"And when ye boys decide about bein' saved, ye jest come an' tell me, ' 'Tis time, Grandma,' an' I'll be on my knees with ye in a flash."

Leroy and me sipped our coffee that was mostly milk and sugar, but it did have a sort of comfort.

Grandma went to get the Bible from beside her bed and said, "Now, heer over in St. Luke, chapter twenty-one, verse eight, ye ken see where Jesus is worryin' about fellers sorta like the new preacher, I

⟨61⟩

reckon.'' Then Grandma read, ''And He said, 'Take
heed that ye be not deceived: for many shall come in
my name . . .' ''

Shutting the Bible, Grandma said, ''I never thought
t' see the day that our little church would be a house
divided. Our own church folks believin' that man.''
She looked like she might start crying, then went on
sadly, ''Well, I reckon the whole world is divided by
war and everything else.'' Then suddenly Grandma
stood up and said, firm, ''Ye know, younguns, yore
grandpa used to say they's times a body has t' take
sides an' fight against things they don't believe. An'
I reckon my turn's done come.''

''What're ya gonna do, Grandma?'' Leroy asked.

''Guess what,'' Grandma said. ''I'm gonna see iffen
an angel sent straight from the Lord likes fried
chicken. Now, ye younguns go t' bed.''

I felt sort of mixed up and said, ''Ye know, Leroy,
I allus thought an angel would make a body feel good,
didn't ye?''

''To tell you the truth, Spud, I never thought of
angels much one way or the other, and it's for sure I
never expected to meet one. I'd have stayed in Detroit
if I'd've known an angel would be here, the way he
scared me.''

"Well, Leroy, iffen I had t' pick an angel of the Lord, I reckon I'd've picked Preacher Rose, 'cause when he talks about God he's real kind and—well, sorta lovin' an' happy. But this angel feller looks like he's gonna spit fire an' git ax mad, like he'd rather slap folks over the head with his Bible than preach from it. But I reckon it ain't up t' folks like me t' question angels, 'cause he's bound t' know what he's s'posed t' do."

"Grandma's questioning him," Leroy laughed.

I laughed, too, saying, "Grandma questions everything on earth and betwixt."

Then Leroy said seriously, "Do you want to go to heaven, Spud?"

"Well, if I had my druthers, I'd druther wait till I was a hundred an' seven, but if the angel is right an' we're supposed t' go soon, then I'll try my best t' go." But I felt bad inside and wished the angel had never come to Arkansas at all.

CHAPTER
EIGHT

After a night's sleep, hellfire worries seemed a long way off, and Christmas worry was on me. Grandma didn't say nothing else about going to the brush arbor or the preacher coming to supper, and I reckon I sort of thought maybe she'd forgotten it. Just the shadow of the preacher remained. Even when I wasn't thinking of him, the new preacher seemed to hang like a shadow over me, just out of eyesight, but allus there.

While we were doing the chores, I said, "Leroy, I jest gotta git Grandma a Christmas. Ye see, she allus had her younguns afore, an'—well, this year she jest has us.''

"I've still got some of the money Mom gave me," Leroy said, then added, "There's hardly nowhere to spend it around here. I'll give you some to buy Grandma a present."

"Thank you, Leroy, but I cain't do that. Ye see, iffen I took yore money it'd be sorta like ye a-buyin' Grandma two presents. I wont her Christmas from me t' be jest mine."

"I get ya," Leroy said, then wrinkled his brow in thought also.

"I could catch some rabbits an' sell their skins t' the crossroads store if ye'll do chores fer me," I said, and Leroy grinned.

"You go right ahead, Spud, and hit the old rabbit trail, and I'll take over here."

"I can't tell ye how much I'm obliged," I said.

Leroy said gruffly, "Just forget it, Spud."

School was out until after the new year, and with Leroy doing my barn chores, I hunted rabbits. First light till dark I hunted. I wrapped my feet in tow sacks, and the bitter blue cold of an Arkansas winter ate at me till my hands got raw and bled and my nose and ears didn't feel like mine at all. I hunted the hollows between the hills, following rabbit tracks to hollow logs and trees with holes in their trunks and old brier patches.

Some days I caught two rabbits, and one day three, and once four. I skinned them and hung the hides to freeze-dry on the barn door, and every day we had fried rabbit, rabbit and dumplings, and more rabbit, and Leroy swore he hopped instead of walked. And all the time I hunted, the distant threat of hellfire and the shadow of the stranger preacher hung over me like the dot of a buzzard high in the sky till I found myself hating the preacher fierce. Yet he fascinated me like a snake charming a chicken, and I had to fight my thoughts so I could keep my mind on Grandma and Christmas.

The day me and Leroy went to the crossroads store, I had eleven rabbit skins and got fifty cents apiece for them. I felt rich and bought Grandma some soft candy 'cause of her not having any teeth, and I got her a store fan for summer with pictures of bright-colored birds on it and thought how, when hot weather came, Grandma could throw her old piece of cardboard away and use her new fan.

When Leroy wasn't looking, I got him a new pair of gloves, wishing fierce I could get me some, but my money had run out.

Leroy got Grandma an apron with a picture of a rooster and a hen on it, and some hairpins that wouldn't never stay in her hair, but I didn't tell him that. He made me go outside while he bought something else, and I knowed it was for me, and it made me all excited inside and feel like looking forward to Christmas.

Leroy had never cut his own Christmas tree and had a lot of fun helping cut ours. He strung as many popcorn strands and cranberries as me and Grandma put together. When the tree was standing in its corner all dressed in red and white, Leroy said it was the most beautiful tree he'd ever seen, and I had to agree with him. Suddenly it was the day before Christmas and there was a tree with gifts under it. And I had thought there would be no Christmas at all this year.

The house smelled of popcorn balls made with molasses, and molasses candy and a big yellow egg cake. There was a plucked hen to bake and cranberries to jell. Cream from the very top of the milk jugs to whip, and pickles from the cellar, and two string-tied gifts under the tree that just had to be for me and Leroy from Grandma.

On Christmas morning there were two more gifts from Detroit that Abe Marshall had brought on a special trip in the mail truck. Leroy's ma had sent us warm socks and red flannel jackets.

Leroy's gift to me was gloves just like I got for him, and we laughed ourselves silly. Grandma just said, "My, oh, my," over and over about her gifts, but her eyes were all shiny pleased. She'd made me and Leroy striped flour sack shirts, and Leroy acted like his had come from the best store in Detroit.

After the feasting was done, Grandma let me and Leroy make snow cream from the thick yellow cream, eggs, sugar, and vanilla, and I did reckon it was the best Christmas ever and me just not expecting it at all. And part of it was 'cause I never thought of the preacher—not once that day.

The Sunday after Christmas there was less people than ever in church, and Brother Rose looked sad and a little hurt, and Grandma looked spittin' mad. After supper she looked at the clock and said, "The brush arbor meetin' ain't over yet by a long shot." Going out the door, she called back, "I'm gonna ask the preacher t' come t' supper t'morrow night. I'm gonna try t' find out jest why he's heer."

After she left, Leroy said, "You think we should have gone with her? I mean, it's dark and all."

"They ain't nothin' in the dark Grandma's afeared

of,'' I said. "Fact o' the matter, things in the dark is more apt t' be afeared o' Grandma.''

"I'll drink to that.'' Leroy laughed and drank the rest of his milk. Then Leroy asked, sort of shamed, "Are you scared, Spud?''

"Well, t' be honest, Leroy, I am plumb past bein' scared. Nigh dead is more like it.''

We both sort of laughed, but we both knowed it wasn't all that funny neither. We were getting ready for bed when Grandma came back, saying, "Well, boys, we got us company a-comin' fer supper t'morrow night.''

I didn't sleep easy that night 'cause flames of hell danced behind my eyes. I could feel Leroy tossing and turning, and I thought, for a Blue Devil, Leroy was as feared of the real one as me.

Suddenly Leroy said, "You know, Spud, I bet Dad wouldn't be afraid of the preacher. And I guess he will half kill me when he comes home, for joining the Blue Devils and not helping Mom as much as I should have.''

"Is he mean?'' I asked.

"Not with me and Mom,'' Leroy said proudly. "But I bet he will be about the bravest man in the war. Ya know, come to think of it, Spud, Dad is a lot like Grandma. I bet he comes home a hero or something.''

"I bet he will, too, Leroy," I said. "I just bet he will.''

Morning made the night before seem like a bad dream. It was 'cause the sun was shining and birds were diving and singing in the clear blue hours, saying spring was a-coming 'fore long. I spent half the day showing Leroy how to chop wood for the cookstove. I mean he didn't know which end of the ax to use.

At dinner Leroy ate beans and corn bread without a word, and I was sort of getting to like him again more and more. And it wasn't nigh as lonesome with him around. Fact of the matter, I figured letting him whip me was worth it just to have him friendly, and I was sort of sorry I'd got him in bad with Tessie. I took a last swipe at the bean juice on my plate with a hunk of corn bread and said, "Grandma, ken me an' Leroy sorta mess around? I mean, the wood is chopped.''

"Well, I reckon so," Grandma said. "But ye be back in plenty o' time fer supper an' gettin yer chores done.''

"We will," me and Leroy promised at the same time. Outside I said, "Rock's afeared of his own shadow, Leroy, but let's take him with us.''

"He is kind of weird—for a dog, I mean,'' Leroy said, patting Rock's head. Rock drooled around us, acting like he wasn't shore whether to stand up or crawl.

"C'mon, Leroy, I'll show ye the creek. It's froze over and we ken skate across it.''

We was walking down a path through the woods when Leroy said out of the clear blue sky, "Ya know, Spud, I wish Mom stayed home like Grandma and didn't work in a war plant.'' Then, sounding real sad, he said, "I wish Dad would come home from this damn war.''

"I never knowed my pa,'' I said shortly, "an' don't know where my ma is.'' I said it to make him feel better, 'cause, truth to tell, I sort of stopped thinking about them a long time ago.

Leroy said, "Well, it just sorta throws a person out of gear to be a family one day, and the next day Dad has gone to war and Mom to work.''

"I'll bet it was real lonesome, Leroy,'' I said, "an' I'm shore glad ye come t' stay with me an' our grandma. Somethin' else. It's good t' have kinfolks, ain't it?'' I grinned big as I could at him to show I meant it, and he grinned back.

Rock played in the snow like a puppy. We rolled

around with him, tossing him in soft snow. He growled and tugged at our pants legs in mock battle, and I thought mebbe I would take him with me more places.

The sun was warm by the time we got to Big Creek, as warm as it had been for a long time. So we ran and slid across the ice, swinging and falling and hanging onto each other, laughing. We sort of forgot about time and had to run partway home. It was bad, too, 'cause it was cold after staying out so long.

Grandma was frying chicken when we got there, so me and Leroy hurried to get the chores done. When company come, Grandma set her best table. The old lace tablecloth was spread. It had turned yellow a long time ago 'cause it had belonged to Grandma's grandma. I think she had brought it from Ireland or something.

Grandma'd molded the butter in the square wooden mold with the clover leaf on top and had it sitting on the blue dish one of her younguns had sent her for Christmas years before. Even our heavy crock dishes looked nice on the tablecloth, but what looked best to me was the big platter of fried chicken and side bowls of mashed 'taters, chicken gravy, canned sugar peas from the garden, and the green apple pie that still

bubbled on the side of the stove, smelling of cinnamon, brown sugar, and butter.

Leroy stared at the food, then at Grandma, saying,
"Boy, if you want to fight *me* this way, you're welcome to, Grandma."

Grandma laughed and said, "I'll tell ye, boy, like
yore grandpa allus said, a body fights with what they
has t' fight with. Now I wont ye both t' heed me right
now. No matter what ye heer me say, ye jest keep
yore mouths hushed, ye heer me?"

Me and Leroy looked at each other, wondering what
Grandma was up to, but we just nodded at her.

"Now ye boys git yore hair slicked down. I heer
the preacher a-comin' up the hill."

The preacher had a nigh brand-new car, a '39 Ford.
I stared at it, open-mouthed, but Leroy was used to
cars of all sorts. I'll tell you this, from the minute
that foreign preacher stepped through our door, things
got stranger and stranger. I mean, Grandma got pink
and flustery-acting, and her tongue nigh dripped pure
honey. But I knowed better than to say anything when
Grandma said not to. 'Sides, me and Leroy watched
the preacher close as we could without rubbing noses
with him, 'cause, truth to tell, we wasn't right sure
he wasn't an angel from the Lord. I mean, grandmas

could be wrong, and it seemed he'd already thrown a spell of sweetness over her.

The preacher smiled real wide at all of us, saying, "God bless us." And Grandma fluttered her rawhide body to the table, saying, "Ye jest set heer, preacher, an' ye be shore t' take all the white meat 'cause we don't keer fer it nohow."

I had to slap my hand over my mouth to keep myself quiet 'cause Grandma told a flat-out lie. I mean, she knowed me and Leroy both were crazy over white. She turned where the preacher couldn't see us and gave me and Leroy a hard look that shushed us clear down in our chairs with our mouths shut.

Grandma asked the blessing herself, which was strange, too. I mean, she'd always asked menfolks to say it before. The preacher looked sort of surprised, too, but he didn't say anything.

As soon as amen was said, Grandma started plying the preacher with the white meat of the chicken, and that bugger took it all. I mean, took it all! Leroy stared at the stranger in awe, but truth to tell, when I saw him take the last piece of white meat, all fear I'd felt or anything else sort of oozed out of me. Guess I figured if he was really an angel sent straight from the Lord, he'd have known I love white meat 'most better than anything in life.

I watched sourly as gravy dripped off his ruddy chin. He sounded mighty human to me as he gulped his coffee with a slurping sound Grandma would have slapped me away from the table for making. I decided to take my chances with Grandma and said, "Mister, are ye really an angel from the Lord?"

He turned a greasy white smile on me and said in a deep voice, "That I am, boy. That I am."

But he must have heard the unbelief in my voice 'cause his pale eyes didn't smile. They pinned me to my chair cold as ice and tied my tongue in knots.

CHAPTER
NINE

Grandma's voice cut in, sort of breaking the spell. "Are ye ready fer yer pie now, preacher? Ye wont hot coffee with it?"

The man nodded and Grandma rushed out to cut the pie. When he was gulping it down, Grandma asked real sweet, "Ye say the Lord sent ye from fer across the sea, Brother Ivor?"

He nodded, washed the last of the pie down with hot coffee, then leaned on his elbows with a sigh, saying, "That He did, Sister Jackson, that He did."

"How come ye speak our language so good,

preacher?'' Grandma asked like she plumb admired him.

"The Lord don't do things in halves, sister," the stranger said seriously. "When He told me t' come heer, He gave me the knowledge t' speak yer tongue."

"Are ye a fereign angel?" Grandma asked, wide-eyed. "I mean, ye bein' from a fer-off place called Russia."

"Angels don't have nationalities, sister," he answered.

"Then iffen that be so, how come He didn't send an angel that was closer t' us? I mean, like one from Kansas or Tennessee, say?"

"'Cause God has special angels fer special jobs," the stranger thundered, whacking his fist on the table, making the dishes rattle, and he stared at Grandma. A body could tell he didn't like her questions atall.

Grandma could tell, too, and she said, near-humble, "Ken ye tell me what the Lord wonts us t' do, preacher?"

"I ken tell ye at the meetin' t'night along with the others that are wise enough t' follow me in what I have t' tell them."

"I didn't know ye were havin' a meetin' t'night, preacher," Grandma said. "I jest reckoned ye'd hold them on Sunday."

"We don't have time t' tarry, Sister Jackson," the preacher said, rising to his feet. "God sent me t' do a job, an' if I am t' save ye people, I must be about my business."

I looked at the empty chicken platter and thought, if he was in such a blamed hurry, why the cat hair didn't he fly instead of drive a car, but I didn't say nothing out loud, 'cause of Grandma acting strange, and Leroy looked nigh as scared as he had the night before.

We watched the preacher out of sight, then Grandma said tiredly, "Well, let's git this mess cleaned up an' git t' the meetin'."

"I'm not goin'." Leroy suddenly spoke loud.

"An' why not, boy?" Grandma snapped.

"'Cause it's hard enough on me eating with an angel, and, Grandma, I don't think I can live through another meeting like the other one. I mean, I was scared."

"Well, ye ken jest rest yer mind, Leroy," Grandma said kindly. "Iffen that man is an angel, I am a milk cow with dancin' shoes."

Me and Leroy both busted out laughing, and I saw the fear leave Leroy. We helped Grandma wash the dishes, then headed toward the brush arbor.

Even knowing how Grandma felt about the new

preacher, I still nigh got carried away, and after him eating all the white meat, too, 'cause the leaping fire made things sort of different, like we wasn't in our own place and time. But mostly it was the preacher's voice. I mean, he sounded like he was telling the truth. I could see Leroy was believing him, too. Grandma wasn't, 'cause she kind of talked to herself under her breath back to the preacher, but not so's he could hear.

The preacher was yelling that people were going to hell, the way he did the other time. He leaned on the stump and told us earnestly that the Japanese and Germans were going to win the war. "They'll take yer land," he said, and paused.

In the pause I heard Jeb Watts say dryly, "Well, iffen they ken make a livin' outa my pile o' rocks, they be welcome," and some of the folks chuckled.

Don't reckon the preacher liked being made light of, 'cause he yelled, "An' they'll make ye slaves."

There was an angry murmur, and one woman wailed, "What're we gonna do, preacher?" and somebody else hollered, "Iffen yer from the Lord, tell us what He wonts us t' do."

The preacher straightened up tall behind the stump and held up his hands to the dark sky and sort of bowed his head like he was listening to somebody we

〈79〉

will give the ones willin' t' follow me time t' sell yer farms an' prepare t' follow t' Glory.''

Some folks shouted, but, truth to tell, some looked as confused as me, and others sort of gloomy. Finally, when the preacher paused long enough, Old Man Morris stood up and said, ''Well, preacher, I reckon I'm too old t' be a slave an' dang nigh too old t' fight, but I ain't too old t' want t' know whar I be goin'.''

''Why, yer goin' t' Glory with the rest o' us.'' The preacher grinned real friendly.

And the old man pulled at his white beard and hooked a thumb in the bib of his overalls, saying, ''I ain't worryin' none about gettin' t' Glory, preacher, 'cause I was saved nigh forty-odd years ago. But what I wont t' know is whar we're gonna live iffen we sell our farms till we get t' Glory.''

''That's a good question, Grandpa,'' the preacher said kindly, and Grandma hissed real low, ''An' I bet ye wished he hadn't asked it.''

To me it seemed the preacher didn't seem to mind, 'cause he said, ''The Lord told me to lead His faithful deeper into the hills an' wait there till He comes t' git us.'' Then the preacher suddenly yelled, ''He don't wont his children t' be slaves. He don't wont ye wor-

kin' fer fereign powers. That's why He sent me t'
lead ye away t' a safe land till He comes t' call us t'
Him.''

After that, there was more standing and milling
about and some folks yelling they'd sell their place as
soon as they could. Fact of the matter, it didn't sound
real bad to me. I mean, no work and just running
around the hills till the Lord said, "Okay, Spud
Tackett, time to come to heaven now.''

I said as much to Grandma as we walked home in
the pale moonlight. Leroy jumped into it, saying,
"Well, Grandma, it seems following an angel of the
Lord would be a lot better than being slaves to somebody. That's why Dad is over there fighting.''

"Well, Leroy," Grandma said dryly, "I don't think
yer dad expects ye t' run t' the hills jest 'cause some
stranger said to, an' I ain't gonna believe we've been
whopped till I git up an' find Germans and Japanese
milkin' ol' Belle.''

Since going to the brush arbor, it seemed to me the
fear of the preacher or hell both came back to me full
force, and I was never free of it long, and then just
mostly when I was around Grandma. She somehow
sort of felt safe. Around New Year it turned bitter

"What's wrong? Ye be sick?" I grabbed his arm, and he looked like a blind person. I pulled and tugged at him, but he didn't even seem to know I was there. I finally got him to the porch, and there he stopped, not saying a word to me, or Grandma, either. Finally Grandma pried his fingers loose from the sheet of paper he was holding and peered at it. Then suddenly she grabbed her chest, and the hills rang with a wail that tore out of her like she'd been ripped apart.

Then she dropped on her knees beside Leroy, holding him, rocking him and moaning. I grabbed up the letter she dropped, and read:

> Dear Son Leroy
>
> I hate to write this letter to you but I have to tell you your dad was killed the 30th of December on German soil. I love you, son, and want to be with you, but I feel it best if I keep working on while I can. For Dad is gone. We'll need all the money I can make. Give your grandma my love, for I know her sorrow is as great as yours and mine. Son, I thank God I still have you. I'll write more later. Until then, remember how much Dad loved you.
>
> Love, Mother.

I dropped the letter and stared at the two people on the porch: the old woman rocking and weeping and the boy hurt so bad he was staring blind. And knowing there was no way I could help either of them, I went to sit beside the cellar in the sun. But no matter how warm the sun was, I felt cold 'cause of Grandma and Leroy's grief. But I couldn't grieve for what I never knew. I mean, Grandma was weeping for her youngest boy and Leroy for his pa, and though he was my blood uncle, I'd never seen him. I just felt bad 'cause Grandma and Leroy did.

Sitting beside the cellar, it seemed to me the faraway war crept close to the Arkansas hills, and I felt more fear, too, thinking maybe the strange preacher was right about the Germans and Japanese coming to make us slaves. For if all our men got killed like Leroy's pa, there wouldn't be nobody to stop them. It seemed the whole world had turned upside down and crossways.

Not liking the way I was feeling, I jumped up and went to the barn for my hoe. I stopped to lay my head for a moment on Belle's warm side. Digging in the frozen ground of the garden the rest of the day, I stayed away from the house, not even stopping for noon dinner.

CHAPTER
TEN

It was dark by the time I got the chores done and went to the house for supper. Grandma was setting the table as usual. I stared at her. She seemed a little smaller, her lips thinner and her cotton candy hair more puffy. It was Leroy who made my mouth drop. He was no longer staring blind. His mouth was tight and his eyes mean looking. I could easily see the Blue Devil gang leader in him.

Neither him nor Grandma spoke to me 'cause they were too busy fighting each other with bad words. Leroy said bitterly, "If you won't sign the papers for me to join the army, I'll run off and do it. I can pass for eighteen. I know I could.''

"I'll not sign and ye'll not run, boy,'' Grandma said, sharper. "Ye'll stay right heer like yer ma wants.''

"Old woman, if you won't let me go and help get them son-of-a-bitches that killed my dad, you'll be sorry, and I mean it,'' Leroy snarled.

"Lyin' an' wontin' t' kill folks ain't gonna bring yore pa back, Leroy, an' ye know it. The best we ken do is try t' go on livin' a Christian life, help our neighbors, an' do our work. Iffen yer pa ken die fer this kind o' life, then I reckon we ken live it.''

With that, Grandma slammed a bowl of beans on the table, and Leroy yelled, "I'll do what I have to do no matter what you say, Grandma!''

Grandma's face set hard as Leroy's, and she leaned on the table and stared him straight in the face. She said, sharp as a wasp sting, "Boy, ye ain't growed up yet. Yer too young t' tell me anythin', anythin' atall.'' Then real gently she said, "Boy, ye ain't old enough t' quit a-shittin' yeller yet.''

Leroy jumped up from the table and ran outside. I started to follow him, but Grandma said, "Spud, ye eat yer supper an' leave him be.''

I was surprised when after supper Grandma said, "Slick yer hair back, boys. We're goin' t' meetin'." I was more surprised when Leroy, without a word, walked around the house and fell in step with us.

Somehow I couldn't keep from slipping under the strange preacher's spell, though I knew Grandma was dead against him. His voice and eyes caught and held me, and he sure sounded like he knowed what he was talking about. I even forgot about him eating the white meat of the chicken all up.

'Cause at the meeting Granny Treat was wailing 'cause her grandboy was dead, killed in the war. And Sarah Jackson had got the news that her husband had been killed. The dark cloud of fear that had been hanging over me since the preacher came flung itself around my body like a cloak, and I could hardly breathe for it.

Knowing Leroy's pa and the others had been killed by the same folks the preacher spoke of made it seem like he was speaking pure truth. With the womenfolks crying and a-wailing in my ears, he pounded the pulpit and thundered, "Ye people have not sold one farm! Ye have not followed the advice the Lord gave me t' give you."

"Not even the good Lord would 'spect us t' find an Arkansan with money t' buy a farm in a year, preacher, let alone ten farms," Ted Sisk called.

Pinning Mister Sisk with his eyes, the preacher said harshly, "The Lord don't wait fer His orders t' be messed around with, Brother Sisk, an' the enemy won't wait either. An' they like t' hurt people in ways an' means that I cannot speak of with women heer. But ye ken think on it."

"We cain't sell our farm, preacher," Miz Morris called. "They ain't nobody got any money t' buy it." The hair suddenly rose on my head as she screamed, "Take muh younguns, preacher, for the love of God take muh younguns! Don't let them be slaves, preacher, or go to hell. They ain't done nothin', preacher. Me an' muh man will have t' stay, but please, in the name of Jesus, take muh younguns." Then she just fell sobbing against Mister Morris's shoulder, a thin bony woman, with her younguns gathered screaming around her, staring fearfully at the preacher in the glow of the campfire flames as if he might eat them or something worse.

"God don't punish little uns or make them fearful neither," Grandma said fiercely. But the preacher drowned her out by saying, "The Lord didn't send me t' listen t' yer excuses. I done told ye what He wonted ye t' do."

Fear and hate warred within me. My eyes were on

⟨91⟩

the preacher, and my ears were full of Miz Morris and her children's keening wails. I could hear Leroy's breath come hissing angrily through his teeth, and my mind shot full of pictures of enemy men beating me with a black snake whip and hooking Grandma to the plow instead of the mule. A scared hate filled me for folks who was going to hurt me and mine 'cause of something we couldn't help in the first place.

Leroy stood up and called, "Preacher, if we go with you to the high hills to wait for the Lord to come and get us, will we sneak out and kill what enemies we can?" The other menfolks stirred—I mean, old menfolks and boys me and Leroy's age, 'cause the other menfolks had 'most all left for the war.

Jed Watts said, "Yep, preacher, the boy's right. We wont t' git our licks in."

"Whether we do any fightin' or not depends on when the Lord comes t' git us."

Truth to tell I couldn't keep from hoping the Lord would wait a right smart spell, but 'course I couldn't say it out loud.

Then the preacher went on, "Ye hurry an' sell yer farms an' bring the money t' me an' we'll decide then how t' fight our enemies."

His voice rang bell-deep, and when he paused to get new wind, Grandma said, "Preacher, it 'pears t' me we ain't gonna have no use atall fer money in heaven, so why bother t' sell the land?''

Most angrily the preacher snapped, ''Sister Jackson, the Lord's ways are not our ways. I jest try t' do what He tells me an' lead ye the way He tells me t' lead ye.''

''What about the folks we sell our farms t', preacher?'' Grandma said stubbornly. ''Ain't our foes apt t' make them slaves?''

''God didn't tell me t' lead them,'' the preacher said sternly. ''He jest tol' me t' take keer o' ye folks. Now, do ye have any more questions, Sister Jackson?''

''Well,'' Grandma said dryly, ''I'd give a peck o' feathers t' know why the Lord picked us special. I mean, it ain't ever' day God sends an angel of Hissen t' the poor folks of Arkansas.''

''The Lord works in mysterious ways, sister!'' the preacher yelled, whacking the pulpit stump with his fist.

Grandma said, real soft, ''In all o' my life this is jest about the strangest I've ever known Him t' do, preacher.'' Then she let her head nod thoughtfully as the preacher yelled and begged for lost sinners to come to the front and follow him.

An awful feeling came over me. I mean, in the

leaping campfire it seemed the whole world had gone mad, my whole world. For it was full of war, leaping devils, and a preacher trying to lead us to the Lord by selling our homes. And I didn't want to leave my home, not for good. Fact of the matter, I didn't want to go to heaven till I was real old like Grandma was. But if the Lord had made up His mind to come get us, I sure didn't want to be left behind, and if the preacher was the only safe person to be with, I'd go with him.

When I rose to my feet, Leroy was already heading for the mourners' bench. I heard Grandma sort of moan, but I didn't stop. I mean, I didn't know this world I lived in any more. But I did know I didn't want to be a slave that got my britches beat with a black snake whip every time somebody I didn't even know felt like it.

When I dropped to my knees at the log for mourners, I nigh dropped on Leroy, who was already kneeling on the ground. And in the firelight his face looked hard and mean, not like a body who was turning their sins over to the Lord. I mean, Leroy was looking like he was going to commit a bad one, not ask forgiveness for the ones he'd already done.

Then I forgot about Leroy. Fact of the matter, when I finally got on my knees, I didn't know what to say, so just ducked my head so folks couldn't see I wasn't praying. I couldn't have anyway, for Granny Treat was shouting in my ears about devils killing her grandboy. After a while folks got quieted down. The preacher said, "Praise the Lord fer the folks that come t' follow Him t' Glory," and shook hands with all of us.

Me and Leroy followed Grandma home in the pale moonlight, and Grandma wasn't saying a word—not till we got home anyways. When we got home, Grandma was hanging Grandpa's hat on a nail on the kitchen wall when I blurted, "Grandma, Grandma, I wish ye'd've joined us. I mean, Grandma, I wont ye t' follow the preacher t' heaven too, same as me an' Leroy."

Turning around and looking at me hard, Grandma said, "Spud, I ain't never been one fer a-followin' nobody but God Hisself. But iffen it will rest yore mind, I'll say this, boy—I got me a hunch I'll see Glory and join Grandpa 'fore that preacher or any-body that follows him does. And the way I'm a-goin' don't take no money nor a-sellin' my home t' git thar, neither."

With that, Grandma stomped into her room and slammed the door.

"I jest wonted her t' come, too," I said to Leroy.

"I didn't 'spect her t' snap my head off."

Leroy didn't say nothing. Fact was, he was still looking mean, thinking about his pa being killed, I reckon, 'cause late that night I heard him crying in his sleep.

At breakfast the next morning I said, "Grandma, 'fore we go with the preacher, I'll chop ye plenty o' wood."

"I'll help you, Spud," Leroy said. I said he could chop the wood.

The next five days passed in a haze of work. Leroy tore into the woodpile, chopping enough wood and stove lengths to last a big family a year. He stacked it on the back porch so Grandma could reach it handy, and it went plumb to the roof.

I hooked the mule to the plow and cleaned the new cornfield still muddy from the first snow. And I even washed all the fruit jars so when canning time came, all Grandma would have to do was boil them. I took a couple of our thirteen dollars and walked to the crossroads store and bought rice, flour, coffee, and sugar for Grandma.

Leroy went with me, and with the ten dollars he had left from what his ma gave him when he left home, he bought Grandma a big sack of jawbreakers and a bucket of peanut butter and another big bucket of white Karo syrup. On the way home we remembered Grandma didn't have no teeth and ate the jaw-breakers ourselves.

When we were at the store, Mr. Satterfield, who owned the store, told some men that the radio said the war was bad, real bad. A man on the radio named Gabriel Heatter said so. Said that the Japanese had a real beautiful woman called Tokyo Rose who was getting our men to leave our army and join theirs like a bunch of flies. Just the sound of her voice made menfolks jump like a flock of chickens on a June bug. And after hearing that kind of talk, I figured it was a blame good thing me and Leroy had decided to follow the preacher while there was still time. But Lord knowed I wished Grandma would go with us.

That night after supper I got the shock of my young life when Grandma said, "Well, boys, ye best pack yore britches 'cause iffen yer goin' t' follow the preacher, ye'd best git started now."

"But—bu—but, Grandma, we was gonna wait till after revival was over," I protested. "Fact o' the matter, Grandma, I ain't real sure where an angel sent from the Lord stays."

"I think ye'll find this one a-livin' like a common

man,'' Grandma said sharply. ''Fact o' the matter,'' she said thoughtfully, ''it might be a lot more learnful fer ye t' see how the preacher lives 'fore ye follow him fer good.''

That night after church, the saddest thing I ever seen in my life was Grandma walking up the road to home by herself in the pale, cold moonlight.

CHAPTER
ELEVEN

I felt uneasy about telling the preacher we'd come to follow him now, and Leroy looked close-faced and mean. But he looked nervous, too. We sat on the back log till most of the folks left for home, then taking the bit between my teeth, I grabbed Leroy's arm and half-dragged him to where the preacher was ready to climb in his car.

I said, my voice breaking a little, "Well, we come t' follow ye, preacher."

I thought he looked mighty unfriendly—for an angel, I mean. But then figured I was nobody to judge, seeing's how I'd never seen one before. "Ye're not 'sposed t' come with me now," he said. "Not until yer grandmother sells the farm."

"Well, she ain't a-sellin' nor a-comin' with ye neither, preacher. But she told us t' come ahead."

"Well, I have more important work t' do now than look after children," he said.

"But ye asked us t' follow ye," I protested.

And Leroy, cool as a cucumber, walked around and slid in on the other side of the car, saying, "You asked us to go and we're goin', preacher, so come on, Spud."

I went and crawled in beside Leroy, putting the sack with our extra britches between my knees. The way the preacher looked when he slid behind the wheel of the car, I figured if he'd been a regular man he'd have cussed. But since he wasn't, I settled back, saying, cheerful as I could, "Where're we goin', preacher?"

"I'm stayin' down at the Davis farm," he said shortly, and reckon my eyes nigh bugged, 'cause if Mister Davis was a plumb black sinner 'cording to folks, it was a bad place for an angel to be. I'd never seen the Davis family, and Grandma said I never would if I waited for them to come to church or visit neighborly 'cause they stayed by themselves in their holler, and unless you was a-comin' to buy bootleg whiskey you'd best be set to run, 'cause even if you could outrun his mean hounds, you had to outrun the old man's buckshot, too.

I peered at the preacher through the dashlight and thought he surely must be from the Lord just like he said, 'cause from tales I'd heard of the Davis family, no ordinary man would have lived in that holler two seconds.

We bumped along the narrow road, more trail than road most times, but after riding in our wagon, riding in the car seemed like floating on a cloud. Leroy must have been thinking sort of the same thing 'cause he suddenly said, "Do you fly much, preacher?"

The preacher acted sort of startled and said, "What the he—uh—" Then he said real quick, "I ken an' could, but while I'm heer I live as a regular man."

Then I said, "Ye talk jest like us, too, don't ye? I mean folks in Russia talk fereign, don't they? How do folks live over yonder?"

"Oh, they live in the cities mostly," the preacher said. "Lots o' people there."

"What do the folks look like?" I asked.

"Oh, like people ever'where," he snapped shortly. So me and Leroy hushed. The thought of little Grandma crept in my mind and made me feel bad, and I hoped our enemies didn't come and make her a slave while we were gone. Then I figured if anybody was going to make Grandma a slave, they'd best bring an extra army with them.

The road dipped nigh straight down, and trees grew close and thick, making the road even more narrow. It was like we were diving into deep black water, the hollow was so dark. After a while the nose of the car tilted level again, and the headlights showed the road filled with dog fennel and low-growing huckleberry bushes. The preacher drove over them, nigh banging our heads on the roof of the car.

We came to a clearing where a house clung to the side of a steep hill and it looked like the smallest push would send it tumbling from its steep perch. The car lights showed the house to be of unpainted boards with a shingle roof. A long, narrow porch covered the whole front of the house, and a sagging railing looked as if it kept folks from falling off the porch years ago, but I'd hate to lean on it now.

When the preacher opened the door of the car, hound dogs came boiling out from under the tall porch, snarling and snapping, more at each other, I think, than us. Suddenly a man's voice called from the porch, "Hesh, ye dogs. Ye hesh up, heer?" and the dogs quieted and slunk back under the porch.

"Who ye got with ye, preacher?" the voice called.

"Jest two boys that wont t' follow me in my work," the preacher called back.

I reckoned to myself that maybe my main purpose in following the preacher was more to save my own neck than to do any of his work, but, of course, I didn't say so. We followed the preacher up the steep rickety steps and inside the house.

A fire burned in a crooked rock fireplace, and it seemed to me the room was working alive with younguns: crawling younguns, just-walking younguns, middle-size younguns, and some old or older than me and Leroy. A huge woman with straw-colored hair slipping out of a bun on her head was sitting in a rocking chair before the fireplace, letting a little bitty baby suck from a naked breast that I could have swore was as big as a watermelon. I glanced at Leroy, and his gaze was glued on the sucking baby, and I knowed he'd never seen nothing like it afore neither.

A girl about fifteen stood in the corner of the fireplace staring at me and Leroy. I figured the woman nursing the baby was her ma, 'cause they had the same color hair, only on the girl it looked soft as new cornsilk. She was better to look at than Tessie Martin. Her eyes were wide and blue, blue like creek water turns when a storm is coming up, sort of blue-green, I reckon. She wasn't fat neither. Staring at her, I wished I'd met her sooner—I mean, I wished we didn't have to follow the preacher on to heaven so quick. Then my heart fell and I knew I'd never stand a chance for the girl to like me, 'cause Leroy was sort of swaggering his way toward her, a funny-looking grin on his face. And she was staring at him like a chicken charmed by a snake.

I forgot about Grandma and being saved, the preacher and everything else, 'cause of pure green envy of Leroy's city britches and shiny black shoes. My toes tried to curl through my shoes into the naked plank floor, and my overalls felt as threadbare as they really were.

Leroy was halfway across the floor to the girl when a voice froze us right on the spot, saying, "Ye jest hold on thar, boy. Ye be welcome t' this heer house, but not t' muh womenfolks—not 'less ye wont a hole in yore chest ye ken stick yer own head through. Ye best not take a'tuther step toward muh gal, Mae Ella, thar.''

I don't think Leroy could have moved if his life depended on it, and fact of the matter, it did. I could barely twist my own neck to stare at the man who stepped into the lamplight. There was no doubt in my mind that he was the man we'd seen walking down our road, and I had no doubt that he was the meanest man in the hills. His voice was the same one that had yelled at the dogs, and I could see in the lamplight that he was a taller man than I'd thought, tall and old with his white beard that came halfway down his bib overalls and his white hair came to his shoulders. The only thing about him that wasn't old was his eyes, and they were a sharp clear blue, and the shotgun he was holding, it was new-looking too, shiny black and pointed square at Leroy.

CHAPTER
TWELVE

"Now, Mister Davis," the preacher said calmly, "jest put yer gun down. I won't let the boys harm yer girl."

"Well, if ye ken handle it, preacher," Mister Davis said, lowering his gun.

I seen Leroy lower the foot he'd been raising to take a step with, too. Then Mister Davis went on. "All the same, preacher, I reckon them boys ken sleep on the porch."

The preacher nodded, and Leroy carefully walked back to where I was standing. We just stood there awhile, then not knowing what else to do, we slid back out the door. For a little while we stood looking off the porch down into the darkest holler I'd ever seen. And I figured if a body fell off the porch, it'd be a good long while 'fore they hit the ground far below.

Breaking the silence, Leroy said in a funny-sounding voice, "Spud, that is the prettiest girl I have ever seen in my life."

He sounded all dreamy, and it made me crosser than two sticks, so I said shortly, "We are gonna freeze our ears off on this heer porch with no covers, Leroy, an' all ye ken think of is a snotty-nose gal."

Leroy just sank down on the porch and pointed his nose at the stars shining through the trees, like he was on a feather bed. I lay down, too, and pictures flashed through my mind: Grandma, the preacher, angels plowing cornfields, shotguns, and blue-green eyes. I dreamed I was running and running and trying to find the peaceful life me and Grandma knew before the Lord sent an angel to lead us. Even in my dreams I wondered why the Lord had waited until now to send one. I mean, there'd been wars before, hadn't there? And in my dreams I asked over and over, "How come?" But I couldn't see who I was talking to.

Now and then the kind face of old Brother Rose drifted in and out of my dreams, and Grandma seemed to be holding off devils with a pitchfork.

I woke up when the sun was barely turning the tops of the trees pink. Leroy was gone. The house was dead quiet, and the preacher's car was gone, too. My hair nigh stood on end, and I wondered if the Lord had come and got everybody while I was asleep.

I walked through the living room to a long low kitchen. There was a large oak table, long benches, and a black cast-iron cookstove. On the stove was a couple of yellow soda biscuits. Shaking the coffeepot, I found a cup of lukewarm coffee, mostly grounds. I ate one of the biscuits, then filled a tin cup that wasn't very clean and drank the coffee, spitting the grounds out the back door.

I watched some straggly chickens pecking around under the trees. The backyard climbed a hill, and on it perched the outhouse and sagging barn. The house was made of oak logs, and long oak logs kept it propped against the side of the steep hill. The heavy soda biscuit settled on my belly like a chunk of lead as I wandered back to the front porch.

I nigh jumped off the porch, the old man scared me so bad. He was sitting in a cane chair with a broken rocker, his feet propped up on the sagging rail. I hadn't expected anybody to be there. I dropped down on the floor beside him and blurted out, "Where's ever'body?"

He leaned over the rail to spit a stream of tobacco juice and said, "My folks all gone t' take keer o' the still. The boy an' the preacher's gone t' jaw with church folks, I reckon."

Mister Davis turned his head and peered at me real sharp, and I noticed his long white beard had yellow streaks of tobacco juice down it and that his bushy white brows looked like large pale caterpillars. Suddenly he snapped, "How come yer a-followin' the preacher, boy?"

For some reason I just blurted out the truth as I saw it, saying, "I don't rightly know, t' tell ye the truth, mister. Seems daytimes I wonder how come I am, but at night at the brush arbor when he's preachin' seems I know why. Ye see, mister, Leroy, that boy that come with us, his pa got killed in the war we're havin'. Seems we didn't have no war till then. An' there was the preacher from a fereign place called Russia sayin' he's an angel sent from the Lord t' lead us right an' save us. An' I have a grandma that don't believe he's an angel atall. So, truth t' tell, I'm sorta mixed up about things." I gave a deep sigh and said, "Mister, I jest don't know much about nothin'. All I do know is iffen I had my druthers I'd druther go t' heaven than hell."

I sat back staring at the old man, and it flabbergasted me to see his eyes twinkling blue sparks, and he said most kindly, "Well, son, I reckon we'd all rather do that." Then he went on. "I ain't never had much truck with religion m'self. Have t' give up makin' the best durn whiskey iffen I did. On the other hand, the Lord allus seemed plumb good t' me. Buried four wives an' they was allus another waitin' an' willin' fer me. God growed younguns an' little younguns an' ain't never been no sheriff found my still. Then outa the clear blue comes this heer fella a-sayin' he's an angel sent t' save us all.

"Nigh shot his—uh, wings off 'fore he could tell me who he was. Thought he was a dang revenuer."

"Are ye gonna hide with him in the hills till we're called t' heaven?" I asked.

"Well, I'll tell ye, boy," the old man said, leaning over to send tobacco juice splattering on the rocks far below. "I ain't never hid from nothin' or nobody in my life. An' I ain't never hid nothin' but my still, an' I cain't see no reason fer a-hidin' now. The way I figger, iffen the good Lord wonts t' come an' git me, he knows whar I be. I'll tell ye, boy, I cain't fer the life o' me figger why he would wont t' send an angel t' devil me about religion nohow.''

The old man looked puzzled and went on. "I allus figgered a man's churchin' was his own choice t' make an' never figgered on Him sendin' somebody after me personal-like. An' from a fer-off place neither.''

"My grandma figgers a lot like ye do, Mister Davis,'' I said, "'cept she won't hold no truck with whiskey makin', 'cept fer medicine. But how are we gonna know? I mean, they ain't none of us had no truck with angels afore that I've heerd tell of.''

"It jest about beats the britches offa me too, boy,'' the old man said, "but I'll tell ye this, all the preachers I've ever knowed likes fried chicken, but this 'n is faster with his fork than any I ever seen afore.''

"Gits all the white meat,'' I said.

"So's I noticed,'' the old man said dryly, then added, "I ain't never been one fer a-followin' nobody m'self, an' reckon at my age I'll jest wait right whar I'm at.

"Still a body cain't take a chance on bein' un-neighborly jest in case the Lord did send him.''

"How come ye ain't been t' our revival meetin's?'' I asked.

"Well, boy, I ain't never been t' no church meetin'

an' figger if I suddenly started now, the Lord would know it was 'cause I was feared an' not 'cause I was a-wontin' t' be there. An' I've allus reckoned that folks ort t' go t' church 'cause they wont t'.''

"Ye know, it's sorta strange, mister," I said, "my grandma has been church-goin' all her life an' ye ain't never been, but ye shore see a lot o' things alike."

"What's his preachin' like? I mean, what do the preacher preach on, boy?" the old man asked, spitting tobacco juice again.

"Well, he says we're gonna be made slaves by the fereigners that's makin' war, an' he says we ort t' all sell our farms an' go t' the hills with him till the Lord comes t' git us.''

"Is that a fact?" the old man said, straightening up in his chair with a thoughtful look on his face.

After a while he said, "Ye know, boy, I ain't never been church-goin', but I done read the Good Book. Truth t' tell, my womenfolks read it t' me 'cause o' me never learnin' t' read, an' pester my brain as I might I cain't recall money bein' needed in heaven.''

"Well, Mister Davis, Grandma sorta thinks the same way, I reckon, but maybe the preacher thinks we need the money t' buy food on in case the Lord don't come an' git us fer a while.''

⟨112⟩

"Still, it 'pears t' me a real honest-to-goodness angel could git around usin' somethin' as common as money," the old man said thoughtfully. Then, his eyes twinkling again, he said, "Boy, I reckon 'tis time this ol' sinner went t' meetin'."

I grinned back at the old man and said, "Ye know, Mister Davis, I don't reckon yer as mean as folks say."

The old man said, real soft-like, "Boy, I ken be the meanest man alive when need be," and I believed him.

The quietness of the hills seemed to burst wide open as the rest of the family came back from the whiskey still. I helped them with their chores whenever I could. I watched the beautiful Mae Ella but didn't get in shotgun range of her. One thing Arkansas had a big supply of was pretty girls, but I reckon Mae Ella was the prettiest I'd ever come across.

Babies seemed to be sleeping every place, and middle younguns were rolling around on the hillside in the snow with the hounds, tumbling each other down the steep slope. Bigger younguns were catching chickens and wringing their necks, and others dipped them in boiling water and plucked the feathers out.

Miz Davis and Mae Ella slammed pots around in the kitchen, and the old man sat in the sun on the porch like he was deep thinking.

The preacher and Leroy came back, and the preacher leaned on the porch talking to Mister Davis. Me and Leroy walked down the hill to sit by a little creek that leaped over rocks and filled deep pools. I looked at Leroy real close but acted like I didn't. He had dark spots under his eyes, but his face looked sort of peaceful—I mean, sort of growed to stillness.

His voice was quiet, too, when he said, "Spud, I've been thinking, and I don't think Dad would have liked me going off and leaving Grandma the way I did. I suppose I was just mad and wanted to hurt somebody or something—just all mixed up. And I'll tell you something else. I don't believe either after listening to the preacher talk again to folks about selling their homes today. I don't believe he's an angel sent from the Lord, Spud." Leroy said earnestly, "The preacher seems a lot like the small-time crooks who hang around pool halls and bars in Detroit where me and the gang hung out some of the time."

"But what about him bein' from Russia, Leroy?" I asked.

"Well, Spud"—Leroy half grinned—"I figured that

people around here have about as much chance seeing a Russian as they do an angel!''

I couldn't keep from laughing with him, but I still felt uneasy. Before I could say anything, Leroy went on, ''I think Dad would want me to help Grandma the way you do, Spud. And maybe when the war is over Mom will come and live with us. I like the woods and streams and not so many people around.''

''Grandma will be right glad t' hear that, Leroy, but what if them enemies come t' make slaves of us?''

''Well, if they do we'll just fight them like Dad did,'' Leroy said with his old cocky way coming back. Then he said, ''Spud, that Davis girl's the prettiest girl I've ever seen, and she's going to be my girl someday.''

An awful feeling came clean up from my toes, and I said, ''Leroy, that girl is gonna be mine when I git older.''

We both rose to our feet and glared at each other. Then the picture of Old Man Davis and his shotgun flashed before my eyes, and I burst out laughing. Sticking out my hand, I said, ''Well, shake, cousin, and reckon the best man will win.''

Leroy laughed, too. I reckon we both figured the years between now and man grown enough to wed was too long to spend fussing over something Old Man Davis wouldn't let neither of us have anyway.

Supper was ready when we climbed up the hill, and there was barely room for me and Leroy to squeeze in on the younguns' crowded benches. Mister Davis sat at the head of the table and the preacher at the foot. Mae Ella and her ma waited on the table.

After the preacher asked the blessing, they passed huge plates of fried chicken, and the old man's eyes twinkled at me when we saw the preacher pick out the white meat. The preacher acted surprised when the old man said he'd just ride along with us to meeting.

I had to sit on Leroy's lap in the car 'cause the old man brought along his shotgun. It was good dark when we got to the brush arbor, and there was already a campfire leaping, throwing weird dancing shadows over the water of the pond.

We were no more than out of the car when the old spooky feeling of dread started coming over me again. I mean, like the preacher was maybe right about everything and Leroy wrong. Me and Leroy walked to the back log, and there sat Grandma, her cotton candy hair waving every which way from under Grandpa's hat. I didn't hardly know what to say, for, truth to tell, there was a shamed feeling in me for leaving her. But she just sounded like Grandma when she said, "Sit down, boys." Before she could say more, there was a sort of strange ripple that came over the people, and we turned to look.

It was Mister Davis. I mean, folks had never seen him in meeting before, and reckon he didn't know where to sit 'cause he was sitting on a log just to the side and a little behind the preacher, and his shotgun was carelessly pointed square at the preacher's belt buckle.

CHAPTER
THIRTEEN

I don't think the preacher noticed the way Mister Davis's shotgun was pointed, or if he did, it didn't seem to bother him much. From the very first, the meeting this night seemed different. First thing was 'cause the preacher rose from behind the stump pulpit, saying, "We will not have a song service this evening because I have somethin' important t' tell ye. Last night while I was talkin' t' the Lord He revealed t' me . . ." The preacher's voice deepened, and he let a long pause settle the people to dead quiet. Then, nigh making me jump off the log, he thundered, "The Lord tol' me that he was tired o' waitin' on a stubborn people!"

Pointing his finger at the people accusingly, he yelled, "A people who hold back. Who wont t' follow but who will not hurry t' do His will. I plead with Him t' give ye one more chance, an' He said two more days. Two days t' sell yer land an' follow me t' the hills t' await His coming." His voice rose even higher as he roared, "Two days between you an' damnation. Two days between you and slavery under the fereign powers. Two days t' choose heaven or hell."

Fear crawled over my body like fire ants. I looked at Leroy, and he had the half-sneer back on his face.

Then the preacher yanked my gaze back to him by yelling, "Two days!" Then, lowering his voice real gentle, he begged, "Men, will ye let yer women, yer wives, yer daughters, yer sisters, yer very own mothers go screamin' int' the flames of hell because ye failed t' follow me as the Lord would have ye do? Would ye? Would ye?"

I felt as if I'd die of fear on the spot, and if the farm had been mine instead of Grandma's I think I'd have given it away for a dollar in order to get Grandma

⟨119⟩

to heaven—and, truth to tell, save my own self at the same time.

Then suddenly all fear left me, for plain as day Grandma giggled. She giggled almost like a girl. And looking at the preacher, I knowed he heard it, too, for he went stiff and his face a mad red. His voice went deep-bell-sounding, and he thundered, "Does someone dare mock an angel of the Lord? A man come to save and lead ye t' heaven?"

Slowly Grandma stood up, and her voice was clear as she said, "Mister, I would never mock an angel of the Lord. But I would an' do laugh in the face of evil men who come in sheep's britches t' lead the flock of Jesus away from His true teaching."

Grandma's voice rose righteously as she said, "Mister, I don't believe yer a Christian, nor an angel, nor even a preacher. I don't claim t' know the ways an' hows of it, but I think ye come t' git money from us sellin' our homes."

The only sound was the campfire popping and the ice cracking on the pond. Then the preacher was yelling, "Sister, ye sit down an' be quiet before ye anger the Lord!"

When the preacher paused, Mister Davis tilted his shotgun at a dead aim in the preacher's middle and said, quiet but clear, "Reckon ye best let the little woman speak up, preach', before ye anger me an' this heer shotgun."

I could see the preacher sort of freeze. Leroy gave an admiring whistle between his teeth for Mister Davis.

Then Grandma said, "Well, mister, all I got left t' say is ye were mighty mistook when ye thought ye could come an' take away our homes an' land in the name of the Lord. Now, I reckon ye thought we was ignorant, an' we may be a mite in some ways. 'Cause ye see, mister," Grandma said with simple dignity, "most times the love of the great God Almighty is *all* we have."

Then Grandma sat down, and I knew I wanted what Grandma had. I wanted the peace and trust of God that she carried in her small person.

When Grandma sat down, Jed Watts yelled, "Amen, Miz Jackson! Amen!" and other folks amened, too.

Then Mister Davis said, "Quiet," and when they were, he rose, keeping the gun on the preacher, and said, "Well, folks, I do declare I had my wonders why the Lord would send an angel t' my house."

A few women giggled, and the men gave some

outright ha-ha's. When they quieted again, Mister
Davis said, "I finally figgered mebbe he come 'cause
he'd heerd no sheriff ever got t' my place. An' I
reckon ye menfolks ken see he gits outa Arkansas
afore he tries t' lead more folks astray."

Mister Davis sort of eased back and disappeared
into the woods as the menfolks surrounded the would-
be preacher. Grandma reached out a hand to me and
Leroy, and we followed her up the hill in the moonlight.

Just before we got to the house, I said, "Grandma,
it's a real bad thing fer men like him t' say he's an
angel from God an' git folks t' follow him. I mean,
Grandma, he was a real bad man, wasn't he?"

"Yes, son, he is a bad man," Grandma said qui-
etly. "Menfolks such as him ken do bad nigh as a
war. And, boys, I reckon folks has followed evil men
since time began an' will keep on bein' fooled by
them till time ends. But if ye'll trust in God an' the
ways o' yer people, the ways o' the Bible, ye'll not
stray off with strangers who enter yer gates t' lead ye
astray, no matter how they tempt ye."

"Grandma, do ye 'call when ye said that when I
was ready t' be saved t' tell ye?"

"Yes, boy," Grandma said kindly.

"Well, fer me the time has come," I said, standing still in the moonlit road.

"An' I reckon they ain't no better place than under God's sky with His moon watchin'," Grandma said. She knelt in the middle of the narrow dirt road. I knelt beside her and, with a break in his voice, Leroy said, "Grandma, it's my time, too," and he dropped to his knees with us.

There is no way for me to explain a heart. I just know that when I rose up in a little while my world was back in its right place and I in mine. I still had a bad feeling about folks following strange men and strange ways, but I knew I'd never do it again, 'cause when we came in the house and I said as much to Grandma, she lit the coal oil lamp and brought her old worn Bible to the table. She opened it and said, "Boys, yore Grandpa used to say, iffen ye will follow the Word of the Lord, ye'll never stray fer off."

I leaned over her shoulder and read where her finger was pointing.

THESSALONIANS II:2:15
Therefore, brethren, stand fast, and hold the traditions which ye have been taught, whether by word, or our epistle.

Then Grandma fixed me and Leroy some pie, saying, "Well, Leroy, I'm sure happy t' see the last o' the Blue Devils around heer."

Me and Leroy laughed, and he said, "Grandma, I'll be an angel from now on."

"Me, too, Grandma," I said.

"Reckon I've had all the dealin's I wont with angels till the good Lord sends fer me t' come home. I'll take the broom handle t' ye iffen ye git over-pious," Grandma said. "Over my dead body ye'll be angels."

About the Author

ROBBIE BRANSCUM has written many award-winning books for young readers based on her rural childhood, including *The Murder of Hound Dog Bates* (Viking). *Spud Tackett and the Angel of Doom* is her thirteenth children's book.

One of five children, Robbie Branscum grew up on a dirt farm deep in the Arkansas hills. She attended a one-room schoolhouse until the seventh grade and completed her education on her own in public libraries. Robbie Branscum now lives on a small farm in Eufaula, Oklahoma, where she writes, and raises calves, chickens, and vegetables.